D0289833

I looked at Myrtle's profile, at her soft easy smile as she snuggled against my shoulder. I did not doubt she was imagining that we were driving away from our own wedding, our own – if I may say so – bigamous wedding. In a way she was right. How much easier it would have been to forget she had a husband whom she must divorce before she could marry me, how much less painful! I sympathised with her. She was not alone either. I pictured all the hosts of bigamists I had read about every Sunday in *The News of the World*. Now I came to think about it, I was puzzled. Myrtle and I could have come out of Caxton Hall and faced the world with ease at last. Mr and Mrs Lunn. All we were asking was the opportunity to make an honest man and woman of ourselves. What *was* wrong with bigamy?

Works by the same author

William Cooper

SCENES FROM
METROPOLITAN
LIFE

Methuen

PR
6005
052
542

A Methuen Paperback

SCENES FROM METROPOLITAN LIFE

ISBN 0 413 53100 7

First published in Great Britain 1982 by
Macmillan London Ltd

Copyright © William Cooper 1982

This edition published 1983
by Methuen London Ltd
11 New Fetter Lane, London EC4P 4EE

Phototypeset by Tradespools Ltd, Frome, Somerset
Printed in Great Britain by
Richard Clay (The Chaucer Press) Ltd, Bungay, Suffolk

This book is sold subject to the condition
that it shall not, by way of trade or otherwise,
be lent, resold, hired out, or otherwise circulated
without the publisher's prior consent in any form of
binding or cover other than that in which it is
published and without a similar condition
including this condition being imposed
on the subsequent purchaser.

Thirty Years After –

This Book
Is Dedicated To
My Darling Daughters

CONTENTS

PART ONE

PART TWO

PART ONE

CHAPTER I

IN A COMMITTEE-ROOM

The windows of the room looked over Parliament Square. I was the first to arrive for the meeting, so I went and looked through them.

It was a bright September afternoon, and the square was greener than one would have expected – also, I observed, less square. Scattered with yellow-grey leaves from St Margaret's plane trees, the stretches of turf shone a damp, lively, autumnal emerald. Round the outside of the square, traffic, like one's blood, circulated all the while in a one-way stream. Scarlet buses, black official cars, khaki official cars, navy-blue taxis, dusty vans labelled *Star* and *Evening Standard,* all reflected a flash of sunlight as they turned the corner and disappeared into Whitehall. Above them big white clouds rode across the sky and a flag floated from Westminster Hall. It was a pretty scene, I thought, in which the prettiest touch of all was that last happy flash of light with which everything disappeared into Whitehall. I was a government official.

Workmen were dismantling the concrete pill-box disguised as a book-stall, which had commanded the entrance to Whitehall. I watched them. It was 1946, the Second World War had been over more than a year: they were dismantling a piece of the past. Next thing, I thought, somebody would be wanting to dismantle our department. I had always had a friendly feeling for the pill-box, partly because I had been deceived by its appearance throughout the whole of 1940, and partly because it signified to me the great flexibility of our national culture – what other nation could so readily think of a book-stall as something from behind which to shoot people?

I heard a door open. It was Robert. Robert was my boss. He

was a government official: he was also a very old friend of mine. I made room for him at my window, a fair amount of room. Robert was tall and had a considerable bay-windowed bulk.

'What are *you* looking at?' His tone was authoritative, natural and lofty, the tone of a man who knows other people may stare through windows but doubts if they can get as much out of it as he would. Robert had great weight of personality.

I glanced at him with amusement and indignation. I was a very different kind of man. Robert ignored my glance. He knew what it was for, and he was far too wily to let on. He examined the scene before us and said:

'Interesting ... what?'

I waited a few moments, and then I pointed across the square. Not seeing at first what I was pointing at, he frowned as if he suspected I was not pointing at anything. I went on pointing. He did see. I watched for the expression on his face. He looked at me out of the corner of his eye, and then he shook his head with a slow grave motion. He had a big handsome head. I shook my head in the same way, copying him.

Sometimes, when two people have known each other very well for a long while, their conversation seems to shed its words, leaving behind for some pairs clearly nothing at all, for others a sustained interplay of emotion into which remarks are thrown more by way of allusion than anything else.

What I had pointed to was the entrance of St Margaret's church, where they had put out a striped awning and a red carpet. A wedding was going to take place. A wedding. I was thirty-six and Robert was forty-one, and neither of us was married. Now you see why no words were needed at that moment to sustain our interplay of emotion.

Robert shook his big handsome head slowly and gravely. He knew it was time he got married.

I shook my head, copying. I knew it was time I too got married.

CHAPTER II

BOWSERS

Another door of the committee-room opened, suddenly. Someone looked in and said:

'No sign of Old Frank?'

Before we could reply the door shut again.

It was a man named James Irskine, and he was referring to his master, Sir Francis Plumer, who was Robert's boss and the head of our division. The room in which we were waiting for the meeting to be held was Sir Francis's office. That is why it had a Turkey carpet, a clock, a large mahogany desk, a hat-stand, and a handsome view over Parliament Square. The room was dusty, yet the mahogany and the carpet gave it a glow. Sir Francis was a Deputy Secretary.

I glanced at Big Ben, and saw that it was still early. Robert, I judged by his eyes, was amused by James and Sir Francis. Robert had large brilliant blue eyes, set in heavy folds of flesh. The rest of his face did not move very much, but his eyes were constantly changing. I was not amused. I said:

'There's absolutely no need for this meeting. The outcome's perfectly obvious before we ever start.'

Robert said: 'My dear Joe, when *will* you learn?'

'Learn what?'

'The way people like to run things.'

'Isn't the outcome perfectly obvious?'

Robert looked impatient.

I said: 'Couldn't you tell this Air Commodore over the telephone exactly what he can have?'

Robert's eye brightened. '*You* could. If he doesn't turn up, would you remember to do that?'

'Why must we have this meeting?'

5

Robert looked through the window. 'Because it's very important to people that they should have their say.' His tone became weighty, as if he were going to formulate an essential principle of life – indeed he was. 'It's one of the most important things to learn for anyone who wants to succeed in affairs. It's very important to people to have their say. They've got to be allowed to have it.' He paused, and looked at me. 'The outcome of most meetings is obvious. But that doesn't mean meetings can be dispensed with. It holds for nearly all human activities – what people enjoy most is not the outcome, it's the way they get to it.'

'Ah,' I said, seeing an opportunity to break the solemnity of the occasion. 'Just like you-know-what.'

Robert turned away, and walked over to Sir Francis's desk. I followed him. We stood looking at the amount of Plumer's work. There were files galore. They were strewn over the desk. There was no need for them to be sorted, because Sir Francis had a stupefyingly accurate memory for where each one was. He never shirked a duty, nor did he ever shirk a file. In my opinion four-fifths of the files we were looking at ought never to have come to his desk at all. I saw one that I had been wanting to deal with for days.

At this moment Sir Francis came in, followed by James Irskine and the Air Commodore.

'I'm so sorry, Robert, if I've kept you waiting. And you, too, Joseph.' Sir Francis smiled at us courteously, speaking in a quick resonant voice. 'It couldn't be helped, of course.' Nobody challenged the 'of course' though Robert's eyes sparkled again.

Sir Francis went briskly to his chair. 'Shall we begin?'

We followed him, and sat down at a long table covered with a slice of dark-blue felt that had been used for curtains during the war. Our places had been laid, with pink blotting-pads set out like table-mats, and ink-stands and rows of new pencils in place of cutlery – all ready for a stately meal of words.

There was always an air of briskness about Sir Francis, incorrigible briskness, to our way of thinking – it reminded one of a terrier. He was a small man, thin and wiry. He was always dressed in a black coat and grey striped trousers. His movements were quick and nervous, and there was something stylised about them. He was inordinately clever. You had only to glance at his face to see that. Under long sandy eyebrows that curled out like antennae, his eyes fairly shone with cleverness. He sometimes held his head on one side with a particularly sagacious expression. Robert and I were devoted to him.

In his official life, Sir Francis Plumer had two passions, one for justice and the other for accuracy. With beautifully co-ordinated formal intelligence, he sought to instal them on this earth. Since they found no observable place among the laws of nature, he had his work cut out.

Contemplating Sir Francis's activities, Robert used to repeat lugubriously 'Not an atom of sense, not one single atom'. In our organisation Robert regarded it as his own special duty to supply the sense, and he did his task with loyalty and affection. Sir Francis had the capacity for making those who worked in personal contact with him feel like that. He was impossible to revere but easy to love.

'Shall we begin?' Sir Francis looked up alertly. His eyes were as sharp and his skin as fresh as a young man's, though he must have been fifty-five. 'I understand the Air Commodore wants to talk to us about bowsers.'

Bowsers – we were there to discuss bowsers. I do not blame you if you do not know what bowsers are: they have little technical and no spiritual significance. They are big motor-vehicles carrying tanks of petrol or oil or water used for filling aeroplanes.

Now please do not think Sir Francis or Robert or I were going to supply the Air Commodore with bowsers. Our rôle was to talk about bowsers. Should you ask, why talk about them required the presence of a Deputy Secretary, a part-time Principal Assistant Secretary (Robert), James Irskine and me and an Air Commodore, you are merely falling into the error of my ways.

At the same time I ought not to give the impression that our aim was foolish or unnecessary.

The government department we were working in had been of great importance during the war, and it was likely to be pretty important during peace-time. The bit of the department of which Sir Francis was head was called a division, but it was more like a small separate unit. Its rather unusual function was to perform what might be called operational research.

What did we do? Take bowsers as an example – though I should like to point out that to us bowsers were very small beer: we were used to talking about machines that were much more impressive, ingenious, romantic and lethal.

The Air Commodore's organisation wanted some bowsers. We had two jobs. The first was to find out how many he wanted, what he wanted to use them for, how many he could manage with if he did not get the number he proposed, whether he was asking for the most suitable type for his purpose, whether he knew if new types were being invented. Our second job was to know what kind of machines various industrial firms could make, how many of them they could make in how long, what new types were being invented in research and development establishments, and whether firms could ever be expected to make *them* or not.

Our function was to collect facts and numbers, and then, through a mixture of science and commonsense, to produce compromises between people who wanted certain things and people who made them.

All of this sounds very well. It might have actually been well if we had been given executive power. But after all our researches, we could neither tell people what they had got to have nor order the things to be made.

CHAPTER III

COMMITTEE AT WORK

The Air Commodore made a preliminary speech. He was a middle-aged man, amiable in a stiff kind of way, dressed in shabby civilian clothes – he was trying to send two sons to Winchester.

The first thing I did was to write at the top of my blotting-pad K.Y.M.S. Robert had taught me to do it at the beginning of every meeting I went to. It was a trick he had picked up from one of his successful colleagues in business before the war.

I looked across at James Irskine. Whenever I looked at James Irskine I was convinced by his bearing that he thought of himself as a perfect specimen of manhood – probably in those words. He was tall, strong and handsome. His body was tall, strong and handsome, and so was his head. He was about my own age. He had a strong intelligence, strong will, strong ambition and strong conceit. In fact he had everything a man could wish for, except a sense of humour.

'I pride myself on my sense of humour,' James would observe in a determined, manly tone.

I wrote K.Y.M.S. once more, and began to listen to what the Air Commodore was saying. His conversation was spattered with letters. He was referring to his bowsers as BW 138s, a code number by which we ourselves usually referred to them. He also had the habit of referring to people by the initial letters of their titles.

'We hope D.O.R.R.S. will agree with our contention,' I heard him saying, and wondered at first what on earth he meant. He meant Sir Francis.

Robert leaned across to see what I had written on my blotting-pad. Whenever one followed Robert's advice, he nodded with lofty, impartial approval. Incidentally, the letters stood for Keep Your Mouth Shut.

'Our overall figure for additional requirement of BW 138s over the next two years,' the Air Commodore was reading from a roneo'd memorandum, 'is 651 by 1st September 1948.'

Sir Francis received the speech without a blink. It seemed to him perfectly reasonable. The figure had been arrived at by calculation, of all methods the most just and accurate.

'I hope that's correct,' he said, brightly. 'Let us see now. You say your monthly requirement averages $27\frac{1}{3}$. Now $23\frac{1}{2}$ times $27\frac{1}{3}$ is' – he paused for not more than five seconds – '$642\frac{1}{3}$.'

The Air Commodore looked irritated.

'$642\frac{1}{3}$ is correct,' said James Irskine, having rapidly worked it out on a slip of paper.

'The figure I have been given is 651,' said the Air Commodore. He began turning over the pages of his memorandum.

'As one-third of a bowser is no use to you,' said Sir Francis, making a triumphant concession to realism, 'we must, of course, say 643.'

'What is the necessity for the other eight?' said James Irskine, menacingly.

The Air Commodore crossly put on a pair of spectacles to find out. His sheets of paper rustled.

Sir Francis said: 'I beg you not to trouble yourself now. I'm sure that in due course you will find an excellent reason for wanting them.'

'Anyway, none of them,' said James, 'exist yet.'

'I think that is hardly the point, James,' said Sir Francis, placing the tips of his fingers together and giving James a look of rebuke. James's face reddened with anger. There was a pause.

'And now, Robert,' said Sir Francis, 'we haven't heard from you.'

Robert roused himself. His fine rectangular forehead had been bent forward and his muscular cheeks very still. He looked at least ten years older than his age.

'I was wondering if there was anything I could usefully say.'

He glanced round the table, and his tone carried such weight that even Sir Francis looked faintly deferential.

Sir Francis recovered from his deference promptly. 'I'm sure there is.'

Robert said: 'It happens that I decided last week that we ought to have a look at BW 138s, 139s, and 152s. Joseph is working on it' – his voice sounded a shade dramatic – 'at this moment.'

'Excellent,' said Sir Francis, all smiles. 'Most opportunely.'

Robert smiled back. When Robert smiled he showed spaces between his front teeth.

The Air Commodore's irritation disappeared.

Sir Francis said happily to him: 'In effect, if your organisation does not get all it wants of one type, it will be able to make up with another.' He turned to Robert. 'I am sure your calculation takes into account the War Office demand we were discussing last week?'

Robert made a gesture with his hand. It was too late. The Air Commodore reared up suddenly.

Sir Francis turned to him: 'Out of fairness, I must not conceal from you, that supplies will not be entirely at your disposal.'

Back came Robert's lugubrious phrase to me: 'Not an atom of sense.'

The Air Commodore was dismayed and angry. Of course Robert's computation had taken the War Office demand into account: of course the total supply would not meet what everybody said they wanted. But nobody could possibly calculate exactly what they did want – the figure 651, if it meant anything at all, meant round about 400: of the 400, any old type would do, and long before the first of September 1948 the programme would be changed.

The Air Commodore wanted to know if we were deluding him. For all his stiff amiability, he was a man of some force of character. His anger and dismay concentrated on Sir Francis.

'Sir Francis, you alarm me! You shake my confidence!'

Immediately, Robert was fully alert and participant. He remained still and even slightly gloomy, but I could tell he had come into action. He made the Air Commodore a long speech, bringing it to a mildly surprising end.

'In all these discussions,' Robert wound up, quietly and with feeling, 'the figure that really signifies is not the number of things your calculating people tell you you need. It's the number that the people who use them can manage with in reasonable contentment.'

Then everybody was silent. It was not the sort of speech D.O.R.R.S. was employed to make. Sir Francis could not possibly have made it, yet he was borne down by it. The Air Commodore, on the other hand, was restored.

'That's all very well,' he said. 'But I've got to go back with something my calculating people will accept.'

Robert said: 'If you'll come back with me to my office, I think we can manage that.'

Now Robert stirred in his chair. I followed suit. Sir Francis was caught momentarily helpless. James Irskine did nothing. The meeting was over.

We all stood up, and a minute or two later Robert and I were escorting the Air Commodore down the corridor. We glanced at each other for the first time. The glance meant one thing – how long could we go on saving Old Frank?

CHAPTER IV

FOND FAREWELL

Myrtle and I looked into each other's faces, into each other's eyes. We did not see very much, because it was an unusually dark night. We were standing on the far end of a platform at Euston station, waiting for it to be time for Myrtle's train to leave. We were beyond where the lighted roof came to an end, beyond where the locomotive stood gurgling and hissing quietly. We had chosen the shadowy lee of a high stack of boxes for our exchange of whispering. The boxes smelt of fish.

'Good night, my sweet...'

'Good night, darling...'

Myrtle looked away without moving her face, and light glimmered on the whites of her eyes. I could just see her lips, long, smooth, relaxed and gently-closed. I kissed her. She fluttered momentarily with surprise. Then she sighed.

I tightened my grip round her waist, and set about kissing her again. After a little while we paused – for breath.

'Good night, darling...'

'Good night, my sweet...'

Myrtle was leaning against me. I found myself looking past the top of her head into the distance. A fog was beginning to rise. In the hazy darkness each of the signals, the green, red, yellow little lights, had a halo, and the glow from all of them seemed to be trying to creep upwards into the sky. We heard the sound of a train entering the station at a distant platform, but it was hidden by a long line of unlighted coaches. There was nobody round about us. The station seemed curiously deserted, and our stretch of platform silent, like an island.

I heard Myrtle say: 'What's the matter, darling?' Her tone

was melancholy.

I shook my head, and went on looking at the signals.

A pause. 'What is it?'

'Nothing.'

Myrtle's hands moved about on my shoulders. I could smell her hair, see her eyes, feel her body – yes, indeed there was something the matter!

What was the matter was quite simple. Unhappily, disclosing it, simple though it was, will spoil my hopes of showing up as the appealing, romantic lover I should have liked to be.

Myrtle lived in a provincial town. She came up to London regularly, but on this day she had come without warning. I had had a dinner engagement which it had been impossible to break – even for love. I had only got away in time to see her off at the station, and we had not been able to go to bed together. I held her in my arms.

'Oh dear,' said Myrtle, 'there *is* something the matter.'

I drew in a breath. I said:

'I wish I'd known you were coming.'

'I couldn't let you know sooner.'

'I know, darling.'

'What difference would it have made?'

I did not reply. I felt slightly ashamed of myself. Perhaps she did not know.

'What difference would it have made?' she repeated softly. With her finger she touched the corner of my mouth.

'What are you doing that for?' I asked.

'I couldn't see it,' she said.

I burst out with the only quotation from Wordsworth I knew.

' "... and oh, The difference to me!" '

Myrtle laughed.

'It's nothing to laugh about,' I said.

Myrtle kissed my chin.

'I'll see you next week,' she said.

'But we've missed tonight!'

'It won't do you any harm,' she said. 'It won't do you any harm at all.'

'You devil!'

Myrtle leaned her head forward. She never wore a hat. She had lovely silky hair, brushed up into curls on top of her head – they touched my nose, and the scent of them filled my nostrils.

'Do you like my new dressing?' came Myrtle's voice. 'I told Rudolf my boy-friend would like it, so he put on lots.'

Rudolf was a fashionable hairdresser's assistant.

'What!' I exclaimed. 'You don't talk to him about your private life, do you?'

'Of course not, darling.'

I knew Myrtle was incapable of conversing forthrightly about her private life. On the other hand, she was very capable of conversing un-forthrightly about such matters. A few allusive sentences, a smirk, a sigh, a lewd click of the tongue.

'Myrtle!' I said.

'I have to be friendly with him, darling.'

That was true. Myrtle had to be friendly with everyone. An unfriendly atmosphere was distasteful, almost painful to her. Myrtle had to be friendly, and really I loved her for it. Even if it led her to speak of me as her boy-friend to a hairdresser's assistant, I would not have changed her. It always seemed to me that far too few people in this world felt they had to be friendly.

'Sweet,' I said.

Myrtle remained motionless.

We heard a whistle blow in the distance. She lifted her head.

'It's all right. It isn't your train, darling.'

From where we stood it was impossible to see the clock. We moved apart and went down the platform. I took out my handkerchief and wiped her lipstick off my mouth.

Myrtle sauntered along, with her fur-coat flying open. She noticed me looking at her, and suddenly smiled questioningly, with a clear flicker of diffidence. She was twenty-nine: she had attractive looks, beautiful clothes, a highly successful career as a commercial artist. Yet a young girl's uncertainty about her charm sometimes overtook her.

'You look beautiful,' I said, and slipped my arm round her waist, under her coat. She was tallish and slender, and she had a small waist. I felt her body moving with a nervous laziness.

The platform was brightly lit, and I glanced at the clock.

A propos of nothing at all, Myrtle said conversationally:

'The week after next, the old b's coming on leave.'

I must now confess that Myrtle's speech was somewhat profane.

By 'the old b' she meant her husband.

CHAPTER V
A QUESTION OF MARRIAGE

I know I was doing something I should not have been doing. I know I was falling hopelessly below the common standards of moral behaviour that everybody sets up for someone else to conform with. I know all that, and I would offer the deepest, humblest excuses – if I thought anybody would accept them. Experience tells me, alas, they would probably not.

My only hope lies in persuading you to wait while I tell the rest of my story. I can assure you the worst disclosure is past. And there is even a chance that unmitigated disfavour may not be my lot when I come to the end.

The story of Myrtle and me had really begun some eight, nearly nine years earlier. Myrtle and I had a love-affair before the war. A very delightful, enjoyable love-affair it was – trust Myrtle for that. For a year or so, actually until the war began, we were lovers. It was one of the happiest years of my youth.

Such being the case, you may ask why Myrtle and I were not married. A question that Myrtle, it later appeared, had not ceased to ask herself for eight years. And a question, I have to admit, that she did not fail to ask me at the time.

My answer is not a very good one. It throws no light on hidden suffering: it reveals no unsuspected tragic events: really it explains nothing. I did not want to be married. That is all there is to it. I just did not want to be married. I cannot say more, and obviously I cannot say less.

Myrtle was not satisfied with my answer. Few girls of twenty-two would have been. We loved each other. She knew that I was not interested in anyone else. My attitude seemed inexplicable. She was inspired to provoke the result she wanted by trying to make me jealous. She succeeded in making me jealous. And I hated myself and her for it – hated her the more of the two, as it happened. At that point the war broke out.

Until the war I had been lodging in the provincial town where Myrtle still lived. We parted. I left the town to go off and do my war service and never to return. The parting caused me sadness and pain. I could not lay claim to universal sympathy because, when all was said and done, I had had my own way. Everyone except Robert pointed that out to me like a shot. I admitted it, although they never explained to my satisfaction why life would have been all jam if I had let Myrtle have her way.

Myrtle and I parted. I relied on Time for consolation, Myrtle relied on promptly marrying somebody else – on marrying the man, in fact, of whom she had made me jealous. A local newspaper reporter, called Dennis Haxby. Myrtle had been Mrs Haxby for several weeks before I heard about the marriage. She had been Mrs Haxby for over five years before I saw her again.

I met Myrtle by accident in the bar of the Savoy Hotel, where I had persuaded Robert to meet me. Robert disliked the Savoy, and as soon as he saw Myrtle signal across to me he finished his drink and slipped away. He had never liked Myrtle.

I made my way through the crowd to her. We embraced, as they say, like long-lost friends. She had a bright look in her eye. She had a new scent. I laughed with pleasure. Then I saw the man who was with her.

Myrtle's companion was not her husband. He was a captain in the American army.

I took one look at the American captain, and at the same instant he took one look at me. It was hate at first sight.

One suffers for one's weaknesses, and I had been directly pricked on one of mine. I had always told myself I did not give a damn about Haxby: I admitted that I did about this man. I ought to have bowed politely and gone away. Instead, I stayed. I ought to have known better.

The American was about the same height as me, and about

the same weight. He had a neat, clean, vigorous, compact look. His uniform was a few degrees fresher than mine. One of his wrists bore an elegant gold identity-bracelet. The other wrist ledged on Myrtle's hip. We wished each other at the opposite ends of the earth. He asked me if I would like a dry Martini, and I said I would.

Myrtle lingered between us with a fluttering, sly, innocent smile. The scene that followed reflects credit on none of us. The American conveyed to me, by tone and gesture, that he had been sleeping with Myrtle. By tone and gesture I conveyed exactly the same to him. Not a single ungentlemanly remark was uttered: not a single ungentlemanly innuendo was left out. I ought to have gone away. He ought to have gone away. Yes, he ought to have gone away. That was just the point. Of a sudden, I passionately wanted Myrtle for myself.

And that is how our love-affair began all over again. Myrtle went on seeing the American frequently during the next few weeks and then he was drafted to Germany. And then she began to see me frequently. He dropped out of the story. It was Myrtle's opinion that we had hated each other because we were alike. I did not care about that. I had Myrtle to myself again.

There is one other thing to be said, one other person to be mentioned. Myrtle's husband. When I met her again in the bar of the Savoy, Haxby was in Naples. He was in the army.

Now Haxby was moved to Rome, and came home on leave at regular intervals. In between, Myrtle was regularly seeing me. Such a state of affairs could not last. With characteristic realism Myrtle saw that it could last until Haxby was demobilised, and he was not due to be demobilised yet.

'The week after next, the old b's coming on leave.'

I did not like the remark, and I was worried by it as I walked down the platform after Myrtle's train had gone. I was beginning to think about marrying Myrtle this time. That meant I now really had got to admit to giving a damn about Haxby.

CHAPTER VI

AN ARTIST'S DILEMMA

When I was debating whether to marry Myrtle, my friends would address me in the derogatory tone which is characteristic of those who profess to love and respect me, saying: 'That's all very well for you, but what is Myrtle supposed to be getting out of it?' My opinion of myself was not so high that the question seemed unreasonable. About Robert I would not say the same. I thought many women would recognise Robert to be a catch.

There was something on a large scale about Robert's nature, in the height, the width, the depth of his wisdom and experience and insight. For fifteen years it had commanded in me love and respect to the point of veneration. That is not why I thought many women would call him a catch. Not at all: there is not much feminine realism in that. Robert also had the capacity for earning large sums of money.

Now the war was over Robert had several offers of jobs in business again, offers so desirable that few people who did not know him could understand why he stayed where he was. Robert had a reason. He wanted to stop being either a business-man or a civil servant – he always had. His greatest desire, his only desire, was to become a writer.

It seemed to me that Robert had some of the most valuable gifts for a writer, and that the sooner he became one the better. But unlike most of his friends, I saw why Robert did not find it so easy to make a break in his career. Why, they asked, if he was chafing passionately to become a writer, did he not do like other artists – hire a garret and write? When I observed that the artists who have starved in garrets have rarely been the kind of men whom people would offer to make managing directors or Permanent Secretaries, I was regarded as an evil influence that prevented Robert solving his dilemma.

CHAPTER VII

HOW TO HELP EACH OTHER

Like Robert, I too wanted to become a writer. Our literary aspirations had grown side by side, and our friendship, to begin with, was a literary comradeship.

Before the war Robert and I had each published three novels with encouraging, if exceedingly modest success. They were the works of our youth. It happened that when the war began we were both completing the first works of our maturity, the sort of books we really put our souls into. They came out in June 1940 while the British army was being driven out of France. The reviews were civil enough. The sales were unspeakable.

We bore up. It seemed to us that life was likely to be mainly a matter of bearing up. This was fortunate, because in due course worse was to befall. We decided that if England won the war (in June 1940 by no means certain to us) and if we survived it (if anything, rather less certain) we would start all over again. The Second World War was fought by Robert and me for England, freedom, and the chance to write novels.

Under literary disaster we bore up. Worse was to befall, and it did not take long about it. It befell us simultaneously in the shape of devastatingly unhappy love-affairs.

It is easy to make light of unhappy love-affairs after they are over. To do us justice Robert and I exerted all our will to make just a shade lighter of them at the time. Just a shade – to us it was that shade which seemed to prevent us cutting our throats. Our literary comradeship changed to something deeper. The comradeship of the rejected, the scorned, the tormented. The comradeship of the hideously miserable.

I will not tell the two stories or describe how and why we fell in love. Each would take a novel – a fact we thanked God we were aware of at the time.

I hated the girl Robert fell in love with. She was very beautiful, but to me she seemed so frigid as to be scarcely human. I used to call her 'The Headlamps', because she had enormous, long-sighted, beautiful grey eyes that threw a light of their own into the distance but appeared to see nothing whatsoever. I was unjust to her, poor creature. Though she tortured Robert mercilessly, she was never happy.

With rather more self-restraint I glumly began to call my own love 'My Last One'. I had a feeling that though my spirit was not broken, my heart was. This was something that could not happen again. She was not particularly beautiful, neither was she particularly cold. She was warm-hearted, snobbish, and frankly brutal – 'I hope you're not still thinking I'll ever marry you, because I shan't.'

Our darkest days of the heart coincided with some of the darkest days of the war, when Robert was certain that we were going to lose. Yet such men were we that the anguish of hearing bad war-news was little beside the anguish of waiting for letters that did not come. We helped each other to bear up. In that I think each of us had something to be proud of. Even in the most hideous depths, we lightened our miseries with a streak of high spirits.

From my side the miseries were lightened also by a streak of devotion to good meals. Robert had a well-developed taste for food, but suffering made him mope and eat nothing. Whenever we contrived to meet in London, I exerted my will to make us go out in search of a delicious luxurious dinner. A trivial pleasure? The only pleasures left to us by our dreadful young women were trivial.

And let me say here and now, that while we were eating our delicious luxurious dinner, I got an additional satisfaction out of thinking about our dreadful young women, miles away – one was in the WRNS, the other in the WAAF – distastefully munching thick sandwiches in their N.A.A.F.I. canteens. The satisfaction of a small man? Have it your own way. Robert was lucky to have a small man about the place. Experience taught me that sexual torment is better sustained on a well-filled stomach than on an empty one.

'My dear Joe,' Robert remarked, with authoritative disdain, 'will nothing break your attachment to homely wisdom?' And then he filled his mouth with whitebait.

'By the time wisdom gets homely, there's usually something in it.'

'Unlike girls.' Robert paused sadly in his eating. 'Unlike girls. . .'

We survived.

When the war ended, I did not have a fine career in business behind me, and was not specially enthusiastic about trying to create one in front. And though I felt bound to exhort Robert to take to a garret for his own good, I had no enthusiasm at all for it myself. Robert, out of kindness of heart, promptly got me my present appropriate and comfortable job with him. Robert had great generosity: when he found himself in a dilemma that laid him open to criticism, he was not above generously landing me in the same.

CHAPTER VIII

AN IVORY CIGARETTE-HOLDER

In the dark days, Robert and I derived repeated minute consolation from dining in the restaurant of the Carlos Hotel. It was small, it was very sedate, and it was luxurious. There was no music, there was no bar. There was no flashy head-waiter with whom one had to be familiar in order to get a table. The servants were elderly. And the cooking was delectable.

We were still frequenting the Carlos after the war had ended.

When Myrtle paid me her next visit to London with due warning, she decided to stay the night and suggested that we should ask Robert to dine with us.

Myrtle was making a deliberate set at Robert. I do not mean that she was trying to make Robert fall in love with her. She was intent on gaining Robert's goodwill. Since the occasion when he had slipped out of the bar at the Savoy when he saw her, Myrtle had made considerable headway. She had gained well over fifty per cent of his goodwill, in my estimation.

During my first love-affair with Myrtle, she and Robert had not got on together. She had been over-awed by him: he had been contemptuous of her. Since then, times had changed.

I had encouraged Myrtle to make Robert give her a drink before dinner. It would nicely fill in her time while I went and played squash. When I arrived at the Carlos I found them already ensconced in the far corner of the lounge, Robert sitting regally on a sofa and Myrtle deep in a big armchair facing him. From the window there slanted the soft light of a fine humid September evening.

I joined them and Myrtle looked up at me.

Myrtle had never played a game of any kind in her life; and she had no sympathy with my enjoyment of athletic activities, none whatever. In the past she had ignored it. Today she looked up at me sweetly and said in her gentle, lightly-modulated voice:

'Did you have a good game, darling?'

With a lurking smile she scrutinised my face, put out her forefinger and stroked away some beads of sweat near the roots of my hair. Times had changed. Times had changed for the better.

A waiter came up to see if I wanted anything to drink. Myrtle picked up her glass. 'Robert has given me a wonderful drink.' She sighed complacently. 'So expensive.'

When the waiter had gone, Robert said: 'Look what Myrtle has given me!'

He handed across to me a small leather case, which I opened. It contained a cigarette-holder.

'Do you like it?'

I did. It was made of ivory, with a beautiful gloss, pale-coloured, lying on a dark-blue silk background.

The waiter came up with my drink. While Robert paid for it, I laid the case down on the table and looked at Myrtle. Myrtle guiltily sipped her drink without looking at me. Robert had his eye on both of us.

'I've always rather wanted a cigarette-holder,' Robert said, in a lofty, detached tone.

I thought nothing would have been easier than to buy one. He had plenty of money.

Robert's tone changed to dolorous.

'Only nobody ever gives me these things. . .'

'Ah! . .' Myrtle made sympathetic sheep's-eyes at him.

There was a pause.

'Robert says I'm the first woman,' said Myrtle, 'who's ever realised how fastidious he is.'

I thought no wonder the atmosphere had been intimate when I arrived. I thought of any speech beginning 'You're the first woman who's ever realised. . .'

'It's true,' Robert was saying, as if his past suffering had been recalled.

That Robert was fastidious was true, though not at first sight apparent. He habitually dressed in rather worn suits, but he had them fastidiously cared for. Myrtle had been observant. Robert smoked, and always removed the nicotine stains from his fingers and his teeth.

'It takes a girl like Myrtle to notice these things,' he said, and he gave me a fine, congratulatory look.

I accepted it.

You may be thinking that when Myrtle and Robert made up to each other I made fun of it, and that when Myrtle made up to me I solemnly took it all in. You are quite right.

I led the way into the dining-room thinking about Myrtle's share of Robert's goodwill. On tonight's showing, fifty per cent was a stupid under-estimate.

CHAPTER IX

AN INTERRUPTED DINNER

The Carlos restaurant was charming. It was panelled in rosy mahogany, and had a high, pleasantly moulded ceiling. The tables were far apart, and there were shaded lamps on those near the walls. There were flowers on our table, three chrysanthemums, with curled pink and bronze petals, in a little silver-plated vase. We sat holding large white menu-cards folded down the middle, and glanced round at the other diners. The room was warm, busy and quiet. We were delighted.

A born aristocrat can have no idea of the innocent pleasure that going up in the world gives to people. Neither Robert, Myrtle nor I had been born to such surroundings. It might have been argued that we were three gifted and clever persons to whom society owed them – we would not have dreamed of taking part in such an odious argument. We sat there, not necessarily remembering where we had come from, but very definitely observing where we had got to, and feeling a modest, naif satisfaction.

In the glow of a lamp, Myrtle's oval face, her round bright eyes and long nose, her dark curls and slender neck made her look exactly like a portrait from the First Empire. And Robert, with his broad forehead, his smooth grey hair and his chin slightly thrust out, looked like a modern statesman – remarkably like Franklyn D. Roosevelt, in fact.

Myrtle ate her soup with relish. She liked food. She liked alcohol more, but she liked food enough. Suddenly I thought of the eating habits of My Last One and The Headlamps – The Headlamps picked a little food and left most of it: My Last One ate a good deal far too quickly. It might have been a familiar glow from the wall, the little silver vase, the sound of a waiter's voice – something took me straight back to the evenings when Robert and I had dined here miserably, solitarily, wishing that our loves were with us. I caught Myrtle's eye, just as she was holding her spoon to her lips. I went on eating my soup. The room was warm and busy and very pleasing.

The evening went by. Robert and I entertained Myrtle with anecdotes about Sir Francis and life in the office. Myrtle told us about goings-on in the advertising business.

Most of Myrtle's talk was aimed at Robert, and I was delighted by her easy confident way with him. When she talked about business nowadays her diffidence fell right away from her. She was still working for the provincial advertising agency in which she had been employed when she first met Robert. But the agency was now so successful that it could have set up in London any time it wanted, and Myrtle knew her work was the basis of its success.

Myrtle had a marked artistic gift, of a strength in excess of what her work called for. I had always wanted her to be a serious artist. But Myrtle had an instinct for worldly success as well. How rarely, I thought, do the two go together! With shrewd feminine simplicity Myrtle had never let her aspirations fall a hairsbreadth outside the range of her talents. How unlike me! I thought – I always doubted whether Myrtle comprehended my kind of aspirations at all. I computed that as a result of her tactics, Myrtle earned as much by provincial standards as I by metropolitan. Myrtle computed the same, and it was clear she thought that until I became the greatest English writer since Shakespeare, there was nothing to choose in our aspirations.

Robert listened to Myrtle's chatter with obvious pleasure. We had come to the end of the meal and he was airing his new cigarette-holder with slightly grandiose aplomb, while Myrtle patently admired him. His face was impassive and his eyes bright.

Myrtle described a dress-show; gilt chairs, glasses of champagne, jewellery, pomade, and the buzz of fashionable voices.

'Cockatoos,' said Robert, hollowly. 'Cockatoos.'

Myrtle smirked at him.

'You wait...' she said, and a look passed between them.

I thought, 'Oho! he's been telling her about his new young woman.'

Robert had not concealed from me that his eye had lighted on someone fresh, but all I knew was that her name was Julia and that she was young and very chic.

'You wait, yourself, my girl,' Robert said. 'She'll probably put your nose out of joint. I think you'll find' – he addressed her as if she were a committee – 'she quite comes up to your own very high standards.'

Myrtle was too happily flattered to be able to form a reply.

'Her name is Julia,' said Robert.

'What's her other name?' said I, seizing the opportunity to face him with a direct question.

'Łempicki-Czyz' said Robert in a preposterously casual tone.

'What?' echoed Myrtle and I.

Robert said it again.

'Is she Polish?' asked Myrtle.

'English,' said Robert. 'Quite English.' He paused. 'She married a Colonel in the Polish army towards the middle of the war. In 1943 actually. At the time when the Polish Third Division was being formed under General Kopanski, to go to Sicily, as you no doubt recall.'

Myrtle was quite unable to recall any such thing and had not the slightest interest in trying.

'Before her marriage I don't know what her name was. His, of course, was Łempicki-Czyz.'

Myrtle and I realised that Robert must have been practising furiously.

'I shall never learn to say it,' said Myrtle.

'It's pronounced,' said Robert, 'as, in English, Wem-peet-skee-Chi-zh.'

Myrtle and I tried laboriously to imitate him. Wem-peet-skee-Chi-zh.

'I believe,' said Robert, 'most English people find it rather easier to call her Julia.' He was teasing us thoroughly. Also he was heading us off further direct questions.

'I'm sorry for Czyz,' said Myrtle. For an instant I thought she was sorry for him because Robert's eye had lighted on his wife. In fact Myrtle was sorry for Czyz because nobody in England could pronounce his name.

'Where is he?' I asked Robert.

Robert answered with an air of mystery. 'It's thought that he's at present in Poland.'

A peculiar expression passed over Myrtle's face. She was probably feeling how much better it was for everybody's sake if a married woman knew where her husband was. 'I should like to meet Julia,' she said, with lingering sympathy.

Robert smiled at her. He removed the cigarette-end from his holder. Myrtle smiled at him. A waiter appeared at his elbow and said: 'Excuse me, sir, you're wanted on the telephone.'

We were all startled.

'Who on earth is it?' I said.

Robert shook his head as he stood up and dropped his napkin on the table.

Myrtle and I looked at each other after he had gone. She was puzzled by my expression. It was the expression of a man who has come to distrust unexpected telephone-calls.

'Oh dear!..' I did not realise I had spoken aloud.

My hand was lying on the table and Myrtle touched it.

'Sweet,' I said. I had not told her all about my past woes.

Myrtle said she thought she would like to drink a brandy.

I ordered some brandies. Robert had not returned. We began to drink them. No sign of Robert. Myrtle and I began to touch hands on the table. We liked brandy. Myrtle pretended to be studying the people round about.

'We'll go home in a taxi, darling,' I said, thinking 'so as not to waste any time.'

Myrtle did not reply. She sensed a faint affront to her natural leisurely pace. She went on looking round the room and holding my hand.

In the end I thought we should have to go and look for Robert.

He returned, hurrying.

'It was Julia,' he said, quite unable to keep a triumphant note out of his voice.

'Robert!' Myrtle was smiling at him, her eyes alight.

I said to him: 'There's some brandy waiting for you.'

Robert picked up his glass. As he raised it to his mouth he glanced at me with a bright, amused look. It clearly meant: 'I'm going to need this, old boy.'

I could scarcely contain my curiosity. A few minutes later he and I were left alone together in the foyer while Myrtle restored her make-up. He could scarcely contain his excitement.

'Out with it,' I said.

'She's going down to Brighton for a weekend. She's asked me to go.'

I whistled.

Robert was buttoning his overcoat. It was a big, handsome black ministerial overcoat.

'Will you go?' I said.

Robert did not reply. He would not have dreamed of replying.

I stared at him.

Suddenly he leaned towards me. 'As a matter of fact, old boy, she said something, and I couldn't believe my ears.'

It was a recognised allusion. Robert held the theory, to which I unreservedly subscribed, that if you thought you heard somebody say something and you could not believe your ears, they most certainly *had* said it.

It was of special significance when you thought you heard someone you hardly knew say: 'Of course we shall be going to bed together.'

Our theory was based strictly on experiment. Each of us could go back with shame and with painful regret to occasions when we had, stupidly, idiotically made the most inept rejoinder of all – '*What* did you say?'

'I just could not believe my ears,' Robert repeated, as if he were deeply shocked, 'I just couldn't.' And I leave it to you to imagine the kind of look we then exchanged.

At this moment Myrtle came up. She glanced from one to

32

the other of us and guessed what was going on. She took my arm.

'Come on, my lad,' she said. 'It's a taxi for you.'

CHAPTER X

GOSSIP IN A CHANGING-ROOM

A few evenings later James Irskine asked me to give him a game of squash. He had a fixed habit of leaving the office punctually, rapidly drinking a bottle of Worthington in the nearest public-house, taking the Tube to Victoria and there catching the 6.20 train to East Ewell – where his wife had ready a meal which made up in heartiness for what it lacked in succulence.

If James broke his routine, it was for something really serious – either need for exercise or desire for private talk about the office. I saw his point of view. Compared with his own existence, mine was chiefly notable for its mixture of loneliness and disorder. On the rare occasions when I judged that James's rather wooden facial expression was indicating a twinge of complacent pity for my lot, I must admit I felt quite sorry for myself. I lived in a small flat in a big tumbledown Georgian house on the Embankment. I was tended by the mean ladylike owner of the house who said she used up all my rations in providing my breakfast. James was right.

We came off the Squash court and sat exhaustedly on one of the benches that lined the walls of the dressing-room. It was a long upholstered seat with a soiled white linen cover. We leaned our backs against the cool painted walls in the spaces between where our clothes hung from pegs up above.

It was a big, low, well-heated room, with wash-basins and mirrors and cupboards. It was underground and it smelt of the sweat of generations. There was an electric fan, which mingled with the smell of sweat the peculiar scent of hair oil in a couple of bottles beside the wash-basins.

I called one of the attendants to bring us some shandies.

James was sitting idly surveying his long straight legs in their neat white naval shorts.

'Have you seen Old Frank's new typist?' he said.

'Not yet.'

'She's told him to call her Lana.'

James was not gifted with a sense of humour, but he was intelligent enough to know that such a thing existed and to work out a sort of substitute.

'She's invented it,' I said.

Sir Francis had delightful courteous manners, but they did not spring spontaneously from the heart. It was his convention to enquire the Christian name of anyone newly appointed to his personal staff and then systematically to use it. James and I took to it naturally enough; but some of the lowly little girls who had been brought up to expect their boss to call them Miss Watson, or whatever it was, even while he was trying to tickle their ears, were put off by Sir Francis's behaving oppositely to the rules – calling them Lana and never even glancing at their noses. And from human contrariness they liked him less for his efforts.

I sipped my shandy. I thought James would shortly be getting down to business. He took off his shoes and socks, put a towel round his shoulders, and said:

'I'm afraid Old Frank is not giving pleasure in certain other quarters.'

I glanced at him. He was showing me an expressionless profile. He went on.

'Robert had a personal triumph with the Air Commodore that afternoon. That sort of thing doesn't do any good in the long run.'

'It saved a row on the spot,' I said, touchily.

'It didn't do Old Frank any good.'

I thought for a moment. 'It's important to remember,' I said, 'that the mood in which a man is going to report back to his boss is not necessarily the mood in which he leaves the committee –'

'I thought I was telling you that.'

'– But that's no reason for not trying to send him away mollified,' I finished up with force.

'Is that merely an expression of loyalty to Robert?' said James. 'Or does it mean something more?' I had annoyed him, and as usual his face began to redden.

'It means that, given Old Frank, I don't see what else any of us can do.'

'You can expect the opposition to start gunning for him.'

'They mustn't get away with it!'

James looked me in the face: '*I* don't want him to go.'

I looked him in the face. We both knew that Sir Francis's fate did not affect James's promotion. James was expressing loyalty to Sir Francis.

'They'll try and use the controversy over A 15s.' As he spoke, James glanced over his shoulder to see if two men wrapped in towels were listening. The controversy over A 15s was highly secret, and we were not supposed ever to refer to them other than by the code-number.

'We're ready for that.'

James kept up his fixed absence of expression.

'We'll keep Plumer out of it,' I said.

'That means keeping *me* out!' Immediately he had spoken James must have wished he had not said it. I was delighted.

As if I had not noticed, I went on. 'Do you know what they're going to do?'

'No.' James shifted his position, as if he were getting stiff. 'I'm going to have a shower.' He stood up, and with the towel still round his shoulders, he abruptly walked off and left me.

At first I thought he had some reason for breaking the conversation. When I first knew him I had looked for hidden significance in all James's manoeuvres. But as time went on I had come to realise that usually there was none. In one sense James Irskine was an interesting man – he was pursuing his career with unusual single-mindedness. On the other hand this pursuit never took him for a moment outside conventional behaviour. It would never have occurred to him to earn promotion by a display of anything other than ambition and rage. So that in another sense James Irskine was a very dull dog.

I went to the showers thinking about Sir Francis and his

enemies. I wondered if James had heard something that he was too stuffily discreet to tell me.

CHAPTER XI

AN UNSUSPECTING MAN

Unfortunately I am not able to disclose what an A 15 was. My own view is that, even for those days, the degree of secrecy with which the controversy was surrounded was exaggeratedly high. However, what an A 15 actually was does not make any difference to the story of what happened to us. Incidentally I suppose I ought to note, since the code-letter A was used for tanks during the Second World War, that the A 15 was not a tank.

To explain the controversy in its simplest terms, I have to say that the machines had been of great importance during the Second World War, were likely to be very important to the country during peacetime, and – there is no use burking the issue – would be of very great importance again were a third world war to begin within the next ten years.

There were several kinds of machines, which had different numbers, and the A 15 was the kind remaining in use since the war – that is to say, everybody was used to it and the industries of the country could readily make it. The A 16, a machine very different in design, was just being developed, and it had to be admitted its designers were not completely certain of it. The controversy was over whether the country should go on making A 15s or not. If you think of the controversy over whether certain kinds of aeroplane should have piston-engines or jet-engines, you will get some idea of the sort of thing we were dealing with.

At the present moment our department, which was largely responsible for the making of A 15s, was inclined to think we ought to stop making them. The other department involved in the controversy was largely responsible for using A 15s, and it wanted to go on.

The function of our office, under Sir Francis Plumer, was to provide relevant factual information, and in no way to try and influence the controversy one way or other. More easily said than done, of course.

Sir Francis had his weaknesses of temperament. His optimistic striving for justice and accuracy earned a good deal of impatience and irritation in his own department, let alone the other one. The other one seized on the weakness, and tried to pretend that it was something quite different – in fact the opposite. From lack of confidence in Sir Francis's judgments it worked round to lack of confidence in his impartiality. That was both serious and dangerous, and as far as we could see, it was undertaken quite unscrupulously.

'You can expect them to start gunning for him.' James Irskine had found out what was in the wind long before Sir Francis had the slightest suspicion. Sir Francis was the last to have the slightest suspicion.

One afternoon Sir Francis's personal assistant said Sir Francis would like me to go and see him in his office at twenty-two minutes past six. Sir Francis met his duty never to shirk a file by working long hours to a minutely planned time-table. This made it impossible for him to see anyone, however important, without an appointment: his own personal staff he could only see after office-hours.

The evening was unusually dark. Outside heavy rain was blowing across Parliament Square and dashing in squalls against the windows. Sir Francis had lit only his desk-lamp: it had a dark green cylindrical shade, and threw a bright glow of light on his papers. Elsewhere the room was in dusk.

Sir Francis greeted me briskly. The down-cast light upon his face seemed to make the lines of age more noticeable. I thought he looked worn.

'I wanted to speak to you in Robert's absence, because what I have to say to you affects both Robert and you. I take it that Robert will not return from his leave in Brighton till next week.'

'I doubt it...'

'The matter is rather urgent. It involves an addition to our staff.'

I was surprised.

'I know that you and Robert are deeply concerned with work on the A 15.' He paused but went on rapidly before I could speak. 'I would have wished that I could take a little more of the load myself. As you see, that is impossible.'

I nodded my head. 'I think Robert and I are managing all right.'

'I don't know how.' Sir Francis looked at me sharply. 'If our volume of work suddenly increases threefold you must be over-burdened.'

It was not a bit of use telling Sir Francis, who gave all his attention to everything, that to Robert and me our work was an alternation of giving more attention to this and markedly less to that. I said:

'In a sense . . .'

'I perceive only one sense,' said Sir Francis. I always imagined he had a high opinion of my intelligence, but at this moment I could not help feeling he thought I was not quite as clever as he would wish me to be.

'Yes,' I said. As he was clearly proposing an increase in staff to lighten the labours of Robert and me, I decided to keep quiet.

'In the ordinary way,' Sir Francis said, 'it would be impossible to persuade our establishment division that we needed an increase of complement. On the other hand our friends who are interested in A 15s have most generously offered to lend us someone for as long as the present emergency lasts.'

Now I kept quiet out of surprise and alarm. Our friends – he ought to have said his enemies. It was an attempt to plant a new man among us to represesent the opposition in our midst.

'I wish to ask you – I wrote immediately to Robert, of course, but I wish to hear your opinion. I wish to ask you if you think there is a place for such a person.'

'Who is it?'

'Dr Chubb. Dr R. A. Chubb.'

I knew him. I did not dislike him. He had struck me as a very ordinary, dim, shrewd, middle-aged engineer.

Sir Francis went on punctiliously: 'It would not affect your own position. Dr Chubb is senior to you, and a permanent member of the service, whereas you are temporary. He would report to Robert, but you would continue to report to Robert, and not to him.'

I could see that really the matter was already settled. Personally, I did not see any need for Chubb.

'I believe we are all agreed,' said Sir Francis, 'that you will need to do a much fuller survey of industrial concerns in connection with A 15s. Robert outlined his plans to me before he went away. Now, Dr Chubb has actually had industrial experience.'

If I was correct Dr Chubb was a Civil servant who had been employed in the outskirts of industry between 1919 and 1926.

The telephone rang. Sir Francis glanced at the clock, excused himself, and answered the telephone.

While he talked I went over to the window and looked out. The rain was still blowing down. Buses and cars seemed to be circulating grimly. Round the square there were lights in odd windows. Sir Francis went on talking.

I was worried. And I was astonished that the manoeuvre was going to come off. Had it been directed against anyone but Sir Francis, I thought our Permanent Secretary would have said flatly No. The trouble was that Sir Francis really did not command the confidence of his own Permanent Secretary.

The telephone conversation came to an end. I turned back. Sir Francis had been standing up, while answering the telephone. He glanced at the clock again, and did not sit down. I saw that my time was up.

Sir Francis said: 'I should like you to let me know your opinion tomorrow. I shall be available between 9.15 and 9.40, and again between 11.45 and 11.55.'

I turned towards the door. Sir Francis walked with me. Our official business being over, his tone suddenly became friendly, almost affectionate.

'I wrote to Robert, putting it all before him. But I told him not to worry about it. I want him to enjoy his leave in Brighton.'

'I expect he will.'

'Shall you go down to see him?'

'Oh, no! Certainly not!'

'I wish you would persuade him to stay longer than a week. I thought he looked quite tired when he left.'

I spoke with gravity. 'Robert puts an unusual amount of . . . psychic energy into everything he does.'

Sir Francis thought, and then cocked his head sagaciously.

'That's a very penetrating observation,' he said. 'Thank you, Joseph.'

With a cordial, faintly stylised gesture, we shook hands.

CHAPTER XII

REFLECTIONS IN THE RAIN

I was disturbed by the prospect of Dr Chubb's arrival, partly because it was a sign of intrigue going against us, but by no means entirely. I decided to walk home along the Embankment in spite of the rain: somehow it was a mild relief to be in motion, however uncomfortable.

The rain was not as heavy as it sounded indoors. It blew in gusts and then seemed to cease for a while. Only the pools of water in the gutters constantly showed a sprinkling of drops. Wet brown leaves were stuck to the pavement, and layers of heavy autumnal cloud moved slowly at different paces across the sky. I felt glum. The fact of the matter is that I did not like the idea of any change.

Irately I invented heavy-footed quips – 'More bosses make harder work', and so on. If Dr Chubb came he would destroy the free-and-easy tenor of our office-life. He would be an intruder. He would demand work to do. People had an idea that work, any work, was a good thing in itself. I wished that I could force everybody who held that theory to observe detachedly for a day the ant-like activity of Sir Francis. And Chubb would intrigue. That was what he would be there for. I did not know him well, but I had no reason to suppose he was different from other men – he had always struck me as rather less clever than some, but that did not mean he was any less likely to want power.

While I strode past the classical grey stone front of the Tate Gallery, my thoughts took a more generalised form – there was no connection, of course. It came to me that I found it hard to sympathise with the struggle for power in affairs. These manoeuvres in our office would produce a negligible impression on whatever decision over the A 15 was emerging. Nobody thought they would. What they would produce were small advances and regressions of prestige for the various individuals concerned. I thought of the time and attention being spent on them. Why, why must they bother to do it at all?

The answer came pat. Because it was their lives, in a way that it was not mine. My heart was in writing books: that was what I thought about, schemed about, and put all my ambition into. And writing books happened to be a solitary occupation, miles away from other people. What their hearts were in, their thoughts and schemes and ambitions, was utterly different – it was in this struggle with each other, right here.

Now all this does not mean that I did not enjoy what power came my way. Far from it. The intrigue made me rage, and I began to think of moves for confounding the people who were trying to get us down. But my rage to me seemed righteous, my moves were designed to prevent the triumph of the wicked. I supposed in that respect I differed not a jot from the men with whom I found it so difficult to identify myself. On the other hand, my moves were not specifically designed to put me forward or put anyone else back. I did not so much want to go forward as to get out.

Suddenly the wind softened and the rain came down in gouts. I was within sight of home and I ran.

To my surprise I found a letter waiting for me from Robert.

My dear Joe,

I have just had a long letter from Old F. in characteristic style. He says he is going to have a talk with you and I presume that he will have had it by now. That is if his time-table has permitted it, which I very much doubt. The gang are trying to persuade him to let them lend us one Dr R. A. Chubb (you remember him, hare-eyed and slightly toothy – incidentally what is he a Doctor of? Letters, do you suppose?) to assist me with the A 15 business. I expect it will upset you, but it's bound to happen and we might do much worse. There is much we can find for him to do that we don't want to do ourselves. I needn't say it will not affect us. I have written to Old F. telling him to accept. I have made a further statesmanlike suggestion that we make use of Dr C's invaluable experience of industry by sending him on a tour of firms immediately. Would you be preparing a list for him? I think a long list, don't you?

Private affairs. Fascinating and v. enjoyable. Julia is a very remarkable woman, even more remarkable than I thought. There is a startling development that I don't want to write about now. I'll tell you when I see you.

Life and art. You are not to worry. In the odd moments in which I've been permitted to indulge my passion for thought, I've been thinking seriously. I've had enough of Old F., Chubb and all others. It's time we abandoned them to their fate. This time next year we must be free.

Ever,
R.

I was comforted.

CHAPTER XIII

TWO FRIENDS

I dined with Robert at his club on the evening he returned from Brighton. I found him standing in the lobby reading a copy of *The Times* which was locked down, like the Bible in the fifteenth century, to a high lectern. He was studying a column on finance.

Two bishops strode across the black and white squared floor and disappeared behind a row of pillars.

'What are *they* doing here?' Robert whispered. It was Saturday night, when they should have been home, preparing for Sunday.

'Up on a forty-eight hour pass,' I whispered back.

Robert shook his head, with the disapproving gesture of a man who does not care to contemplate such things, and dignifiedly walked towards a small room where we could drink a glass of sherry. I followed him.

We sat down on leather-covered armchairs in a corner. The club was deserted, and the only other person in the room was a dozing whiskery old man who looked like a retired professor of zoology. The room was in a corner of the building, and had windows on two sides: through them shone bands of lemon-coloured evening sky.

I watched Robert while he was ordering the sherry.

'You look very well,' I said.

His face had a relaxed glow and his eyes were sparkling. The chocolate-coloured stains which often showed below his eyes had lightened. He did not reply. I was waiting to be told the startling development.

'Well?' I said, when the waiter had gone away.

Robert sipped his sherry. Then he said:

'Julia wants me to marry her.'

I was completely taken aback.

'When?' I asked, incredulously.

'As soon as possible.'

'Will you?' I went on, even forgetting he would certainly not reply.

Robert smiled to himself. I could see that he was very happy.

Suddenly it occurred to me that I had not felt a rush of pleasure or satisfaction on his behalf. I was ashamed of myself. I had not felt a rush of pleasure on his behalf because I was envious and jealous.

'What about her husband?' I said.

'She says she'd stopped living with him before he went back to Poland.'

'Is she divorcing him?'

'As far as I know.'

'Don't you know?'

Robert glanced at me, surprised by my tone.

'There's some mystery about it,' he said, 'which I propose to solve.' He smiled at me. I guessed that he understood what was the matter with me.

We were silent for a little while. The strain seemed to be released. I said: 'That will keep you occupied.'

'Occupied?' Robert said. He looked away, with a particular glimmer in his eye. 'I've never been so occupied in my life before. Never! ...'

We lapsed into concupiscent imagining.

'Honestly, old boy,' he said. 'A week's about as much as I'm good for. All the time.'

'And you think of marriage!' said I.

Robert said promptly: 'That wouldn't be all the time.'

'H'm,' I said.

'She's considered that.'

'Well, well ...'

'She wants me to give her five children, straight away.'

'All at once?'

'She thinks that will be the perfect solution.'

'It's a solution, all right,' I said. 'But it sounds

comprehensive rather than perfect. Where would you keep them all?'

'I don't know,' said Robert. 'You must help me. I'll have to buy a house somewhere.' There was just a shade of the grandiose in his tone.

'A very big one,' I said.

'I suppose it will cost rather a lot?'

'Yes, but you can afford it,' I said. During his years in business Robert had saved quite a lot of money, but he always cagily prevented me from finding out how much.

'I'm afraid she has rather expensive tastes.' He checked himself. 'No. That is not correct.' He smiled. 'Very expensive tastes.' He glanced at me, and immediately gave away that Julia's expensive tastes were sweetly flattering to him.

I remained silent for a while. I ought to have been able to say I hoped he had found great happiness at last. I said:

'It really is fantastic.'

Robert nodded.

'How long has it taken all this to happen?' I said.

'About a month.'

Our glasses were empty. Robert picked up his, and twisted it round by the stem.

His tone was deep and perfectly natural. He said: 'It really does look as if she's fallen in love.'

I took his word for it, and I had none of the sharp revulsion of feeling that such a statement seemed to evoke in other people. When Robert said: 'It really does look as if she's fallen in love,' he was being neither boastful nor patronising. You must take my word for that. Neither, I must admit, was he showing any sign of blowing his brains out.

'I'm glad,' I said. I recalled the days of The Headlamps, and I thought of now. Affection swept away my jealousy. 'Perhaps your luck's changed.'

Robert said: 'Perhaps it's changed for you too, old boy.'

My own luck. 'Myrtle?' I said, with a feeling of tenderness and relief.

Robert did not speak.

'Tell me about Julia!'

'You must meet her. I want you to meet her.' He put down

48

the glass again and looked at me. 'She's a remarkable woman. And she's very attractive to look at.' Suddenly he came out with one of his surprising uninnocent franknesses. 'She's got a very beautiful body...'

I, who could easily have given a complete anatomical description of one of my loves, felt slightly embarrassed.

Robert glanced at his watch. 'Are you feeling hungry?'

I had been hoping for another glass of sherry, but nothing could make me lie about not being hungry.

We stood up. The whiskery old man was still dozing. The yellow light in the windows had faded. The newspapers on the tables looked tatty and abandoned. I let Robert lead the way.

I suddenly recalled my pang of jealousy and envy. I was ashamed, although I accepted it. For I knew that friendship, however free, however undemanding, gave rise to such outbursts. This outburst had done no damage. I doubted if it was the last.

CHAPTER XIV

BY THE SERPENTINE

The following Sunday afternoon Robert and I walked across Hyde Park. It was a beautiful day. The sun shone brilliantly, without heat, from a cloudless sky of purest blue. The glare of summer had gone, leaving the serene freshness of autumn, serene freshness such as was supposed to come in the autumn of life as well – I saw little prospect of it in my own.

We met at Marble Arch and crossed over to the avenue of still leafy trees, skirting the crowds of people, chiefly men, who were listening to the weekend orators, and making our way to the wide stretches of grass. There was a light steady breeze. We passed a little boy and his father who were preparing to fly a kite, a delicately-constructed box-kite made of pink and yellow paper, which instantly took one's imagination away to China, far, far away. And we passed numerous couples lying on the grass, who had taken off their jackets and undone their blouses for an afternoon's enjoyment of the erotic kiss – which brought one's imagination swiftly home again.

My scientific curiosity was aroused. 'Some of them,' I said to Robert, 'seem to kiss each other all afternoon without stopping.' I felt that Robert, in his rôle of pundit, ought to have some explanation of how they managed to keep it up.

We were making for the Serpentine. The ground sloped down before us, giving an air of spaciousness. In the distance, a long way away on the other side of the lake, there was a high, dark, hazy mass of trees and rising above it the fantastic pinnacles of Knightsbridge and Kensington. All this space! one felt – and it is only a small part of the great city stretching beyond on all sides. London lies horizontal, open to the sky.

'When is Myrtle coming up again?' Robert asked.

'Next weekend.'

I did not go on with the conversation, because it was painful to me. Haxby was on leave. This weekend Myrtle was with him. I could not bear to think of it.

We walked steadily. The grass was thick and brownish-green. We could now see the glitter of water and the dark shapes of rowing-boats on it.

'I could get on with Myrtle very well,' said Robert. There was an amused reminiscent gleam in his eye.

'What's she been saying to you?'

'Nothing in particular.' He turned to me. 'You always think we've been saying something particularly significant to each other. That's far from the case.' He looked away again, and his tone of voice deepened a little. 'Myrtle and I understand each other. That's all. Don't ask me why.'

'Very nice, too,' I said, feeling I had been left out of something.

'Don't be absurd!' Robert laughed affectionately. He became serious again. 'You could do much worse than marry Myrtle.'

I considered the comparison.

Robert said: 'She's kind and affectionate, and she loves you. In her way she's quite a remarkable woman. She's quite clever and she's damned shrewd. She has a simple, earthy idea of what men are like and what they want – '

'Well, I'm damned!' I interrupted.

Robert looked surprised

'As if I didn't know all that!' I said. 'As if I couldn't have told *you* that. Eight years ago! In the days when you were saying your remarks bounced off her forehead.'

Robert looked hurt. He hated to be reminded of his mistakes in human judgment, and, given half a chance, tried to pretend he had never made them.

'You talk as if she were your discovery,' I said.

Robert shook his head, as if it were useless to go on talking to anyone so unreasonable.

I said: 'The fact of the matter is, you don't credit anybody else with being able to see what Myrtle's like as well as you can yourself.'

Robert walked a few steps in silence.

'That is true,' he said.

The apologetic reply would have done no good with me, but the colossal I could never resist. I gave in.

By this time we were nearly at the water's edge. The lake was a pretty sight. The breeze was still blowing, stirring the surface into tiny waves. The bank was lined with spectators, watching the row-boats – expecting them to collide and preparing to enjoy the excitement of seeing somebody fall overboard.

As usual there were boats containing sailors, who, one would have thought, saw enough of the water while they were on duty; there were boats containing giggling, incompetent girls wearing trousers; there were boats containing guardsmen, who called oafishly all the time; there were boats containing family-parties obviously exasperated with each other; and, to our delight, there was a boat-load of Indians, looking dusky, garrulous and cold.

I assumed that Robert thought I intended to marry Myrtle, and, as far as he would permit himself, was encouraging me – we were much too chary to give each other direct advice. Everything he had said about Myrtle was true. That I could do much worse than marry her I knew very well. The time had come for me to make up my mind.

In a little while we were passing the queue of people waiting to hire boats. They sat on rows of chairs, four deep, beside the water: every time the top chairs became empty they all moved up. They appeared to sit there for hours, and were therefore the subject of disapproving comment by passers-by. It seemed to me characteristic of passers-by, that their powers of observation ranged from the meanly small to the frankly negative. Anyone with half an eye could see the queue was alight with romance. Many of its members were comely, all of them were out for a good time. The chairs set them in a perfect position for flirting with strangers right and left. No wonder they sat there for hours!

We walked on a little further and sat down to talk on chairs facing the water. We began to talk about Myrtle again. Robert must have been having one of his long allusive conversations with her on her last visit. He now had no doubt that she had always been in love with me.

I said, perfectly sincerely: 'It's extraordinary. I can't think why.'

Robert said: 'You appear to be her romantic ideal, that's all.'

'Did she actually say that?'

'Of course not!'

'It's ridiculous.'

Robert grinned. 'There it is, old boy. There's no question of it. You're her romantic ideal.'

I thought it over.

At last I said: 'It's curious she and Haxby have not had any children.'

Robert glanced at me.

'She did tell me that – not in so many words, of course.' He paused.

I stared at him.

Robert said: 'It appears that you are the only man she's ever wanted to have children by.'

I could not reply. At that moment I decided to marry Myrtle.

CHAPTER XV

AN UNUSUAL PROPOSAL

One of the things that really did surprise me, when I began to find out what people in the metropolis did, was the frequency with which they proposed marriage to each other when one or both parties already had a spouse.

I felt as if my upbringing had been peculiarly – and unnecessarily – conscribed. With juvenile desire to have everything cut-and-dried, to see everything as black or white, I had imagined that people who were already married automatically could not make or receive further proposals. How wrong I was!

Things that other people do very properly surprise and shock us. And then time flows, the wheel turns .... and we do those very things ourselves. Or perhaps I should do better to speak purely for myself and say that I did.

I had decided to marry Myrtle after all. Earlier I hinted to you that I would tell the story of a modest attempt to atone for misbehaviour. That was from your point of view. It weighed with me, but, like someone else's point of view, rather less than my own. I wanted to marry, I wanted to have children, I wanted Myrtle for my wife.

I gave some thought to my proposal.

The general convention, that a man shall propose marriage to a woman *before* going to bed with her, had never appealed to me. I know I shall give offence, but I must be frank. The general convention had to me always smacked of a rather crude bargain. How much nicer it would be, I had always thought, how much more graceful and profound a compliment to propose *after*.

I decided to propose to Myrtle after, immediately after.

And so I waited for Myrtle's next visit with powerfully growing emotion. I imagined the scene. I wondered what she would say. Eight years she had been in love. I imagined her lazy fluttering look in collapse when she heard me propose – in soft, happy, lingering collapse.

And so the evening came round. I met Myrtle, and took her to dine at the Carlos. I bought her the expensive drinks Robert had given her a taste for. She was often rather low-spirited; tonight she was not. Her business in London had been successful. She was wearing a new elegant black dress – goodness knows where she had acquired the coupons for it. Rudolf had expended great art on her hair. She touched the beautifully arranged curls.

'I suppose it's a complete waste of money,' she said, with a lubricious sigh.

I nodded, happily.

Over dinner she asked me about Robert and Julia.

'The sly old thing,' she said.

I observed that I had not yet been allowed to meet Julia. I said:

'He's keeping her to himself.'

'I don't blame him,' said Myrtle.

We held hands across the table.

'Darling,' I said.

Myrtle sighed.

The question of drinking brandy arose. With my eye fixed on the great moment, I said:

'I've got some whisky in the flat.' Myrtle was very fond of whisky, and as it was hard to get I hoarded it for her visits.

'Why not have whisky *and* brandy?' she said.

In the taxi I kissed her. And Myrtle kissed me.

My flat was on the second floor, and it looked over the river. We stood by the bedroom window and paused for a moment. The water was high, and although the night was very dark the surface was illumined with a mysterious patch of grey light. There was very little traffic along the road, and we could hear the trees rustling.

Myrtle, standing beside me, sighed and raised her arms to the window sash. It was simply asking me to slip my hands under her breasts.

'Wonderful hair,' I whispered, pushing my nose through her curls. She laughed and turned her head back.

I drew the curtains and switched on the lamp. It was a furnished flat, and the room had little charm. All the same the glow of the lamp looked soft and inviting. Myrtle's elegant new dress seemed to slip off very simply. I kissed her shoulder with delight.

I remembered the whisky I had promised her. When I came back from the living room, Myrtle was lying in bed. Her eyes were bright and her cheeks pink. She watched me bring some water from the wash-basin. I poured some whisky into two glasses and sat on the bed beside her.

'Fancy going to bed with a whisky-bottle,' she said, and took a healthy sip.

I saw nothing wrong with it. I was not as young as I used to be. I took a healthy sip, and ran my hand down her side. We both sipped again. Her flesh had a beautiful sheen. I put down my glass. I took Myrtle's glass away from her: she dropped her eyelids as if she did not know why. The whole room seemed to give a sudden flicker.

For a time I forgot that I intended to propose marriage.

However, in due course, I remembered the great moment again. Shall I, now? I wondered. Now, or in a little while? Now? I lifted myself up a little, so that I could look at Myrtle's face. Her eyes were closed. I felt the joy of possessing. The long smooth lips, the dark pretty eyebrows – there was a gleam of sweat on her forehead. Now.

'Darling,' I said. 'There's something I want to ask you.'

Myrtle's eyes opened, wide.

'Darling,' I said. 'Will you marry me?'

And I heard her sweet, lightly-modulated voice say: 'What, me?'

PART II

CHAPTER I

AT A PARTY FOR POLES

A t last I was allowed to meet Julia.
    One evening at the beginning of October, Myrtle and I were invited to a cocktail party, given by an Anglo-Polish society, mainly for Polish officers. Julia was employed as its secretary.

'Shall we meet Mr Łempicki-Czyz?' Myrtle asked.

The idea of absent husbands was constantly with us. Myrtle had promised to become my wife, so I can tell you that to a prospective husband the beloved's present spouse, even when he is absent, looms in the imagination like the Rock of Gibraltar – and if you should happen not to have seen the Rock of Gibraltar, let me explain that it is a thoroughly unprepossessing rock.

The party was held in a house at the lower end of South Audley Street. Julia's society had the first floor, and for the party a room which ran the full width of the house had been beautifully decorated. There were three tall french windows opening on to a narrow balcony with a wrought iron balustrade: the room must normally have been rather dark, for the walls were painted dark green and the houses opposite were near. Tonight, in the centre of each wall glowed an exquisite bas-relief medallion moulded in white cartridge paper: the artistry was dazzling, of the pale convoluted shapes with their light shadows and clear edges. The only flowers were bunches of asters, in white, carmine and purple-blue. And there were male Polish faces, some of them startlingly powerful – oval, with strong cheek-bones and cleft chins; broad, unusually flat faces with brilliant narrow eyes – some of them startlingly powerful, and some of them, to my mind, startlingly crazy.

When Myrtle and I reached the top of the staircase of the house, we were so late that the reception committee had temporarily gone off duty. Loud and cheerful talk came from the room, and a crowd of people stood in the doorway. Myrtle and I hesitated. A young woman suddenly came to us out of the crowd.

'I'm Julia.'

'That's very clever of you.'

'I made Robert describe you.' She looked at me with a bright, furtive, amused glint in her eye. It was such a strong glint that I suddenly found myself feeling bright, furtive and amused, too.

We shook hands.

'I expect you'd like something to drink.' She cast a bright, furtive, slightly less amused glance at Myrtle, and then looked at a point somewhere in between us, as she said: 'I'm afraid I've had an awful lot already.' She shook her head, and her loose silky hair swung against her cheeks. 'Let me take you to the bar.'

Myrtle had an eager, happy expression as we plunged through the crowd. I held her hand. As a matter of fact my other hand was being held by Julia, so that we should not get separated, of course. The room had a sort of glow, the sort of glow that any room has when it is filled by a party and everyone happens already to be slightly under the influence of alcohol.

I heard Julia saying: 'There's some wonderful Polish drink and lots of lovely bits of food. Personally, I go for the drink.'

I looked her up and down and thought 'Yes, I don't suppose you're much of a one for the food.' She had a lean nervous look. To care for food you have to be able to relax a bit. On the other hand she did look as if she was one for the drink.

I glanced around the room. It was then that I noticed the white medallions shining on the walls: there were only a few lamps, placed cunningly to illuminate them. I noticed the small knots of red, white and blue flowers, and the strange Polish men's faces.

'What do you think of it?' said Julia.

Myrtle replied to her, and I did not join in the conversation. I was having my first good look at Julia.

There was no doubt that Julia was a beautiful young woman, and though I had already taken Robert's word for it, I was happy to make the judgment for myself. She was tall and lean and active. Her hips were narrow, but her breasts were remarkably full and shapely. She had fair silky hair cut above her shoulders, and big, slightly protruding grey eyes. Her forehead was broad and her chin pointed: while talking to you she bent her head down a little and the impression you got was of big eyes, bright with amusement, coming at you. She talked to Myrtle while I stared at her.

'I do drawings for advertising,' I heard Myrtle saying, in a melancholy tone.

I remembered that Robert had told me Julia was chic, and I observed this to be true. She was dressed in the height of fashion. The effect was of plain elegance, differing from Myrtle's elegance, which, in spite of an equally plain dress, was a shade theatrical.

'You need another drink.' Julia turned to me suddenly, and I could have sworn she let her bosom brush against my arm. And I for my part have to admit that I did not move my arm away.

While Julia was speaking to the barman in Polish, I reflected that it is a very rare woman who can have a lot of alcohol and a lot of men without it showing somewhere. I was looking at her throat, where I thought her skin, under the layer of powder, showed a warm reddish coarsening. It was not beautiful. Yet it was attractive, because it told one that one could let oneself go.

Julia handed me my glass.

'Who's Robert talking to?' I said. I had seen him in the corner of the room, talking with the sort of affable weightiness he always displayed to strangers at parties.

Julia did not need to look. 'The general and the minister.' She gave me a knowing grin. 'Of course.'

I shook my head. 'He would.'

'He's a darling, all the same. I expect he's telling them what a wonderful secretary the society has.' Suddenly she looked at me, and said with a deep constrained force: 'Robert is a wonderful man, isn't he?'

I was taken aback by her change in tone. She was watching me. She leaned a little closer, and said in a low voice, almost whispering:

'I want you to help me.'

For an instant she searched in my face; and then as if she were afraid to risk finding an answer, she looked away. Her eyes had suddenly taken on a heightened sheen, and her head was bent. She was in love with him. I knew that somehow she was feeling a wave of romantic hope.

I could not say anything.

Julia looked up again. The moment of revelation had passed. Her eyes were glinting again with amusement. She said:

'He doesn't want me to lose my job.'

'There's nobody better than Robert at helping one to keep one's job.'

'Are you an outcast, too?'

I said: 'Not that I know of.'

'I can't imagine why he should want me to keep the job. They pay me practically nothing, Joe, practically nothing.'

'How much?'

Julia gave me a nervous direct look. 'Five pounds a week.'

I imagined the response of Myrtle or Robert to such a direct question. As Julia replied I caught the expression on Myrtle's face, round-eyed and shrewdly innocent. Five pounds a week! Myrtle made more like twenty.

I was about to say something, when Robert beckoned across the room to Julia.

'I must leave you for a moment.' She moved away, and then turned back, looking at me and ignoring Myrtle. 'Please, don't go.' Her voice became urgent. 'There's something I simply must tell you.'

CHAPTER II

AMBUSHES AND HUSBANDS

I watched Julia, and said to Myrtle: 'What do you think of her?'

'I think she's very clever, darling.' Myrtle's tone was distinctly melancholy again. She looked at me. 'What are you laughing at?'

'Just your show of . . . bogus inferiority.'

'It isn't bogus!' Myrtle looked as if she were struggling with a desperate drawback. 'Did you notice how fluently she spoke Polish?'

'Did you, darling, notice she was only earning five pounds a week?'

Myrtle could not resist a complacent smirk. 'Well, there is that,' she said, doubtfully.

I touched my glass against hers.

'You're a wonderful woman.'

Myrtle softened. With a feeble effort at composure, she said: 'So I'm a wonderful woman, eh?'

I felt a strong burst of emotion.

'The sooner you're *my* woman the better.'

I was slightly drunk, and I did not keep a pressing note out of my voice.

'Oh, darling!' Myrtle was upset.

'I'm sorry, darling.' I took hold of her hand.

Myrtle's fingers tightened in mine.

'I mean it, darling,' I said unrestrainedly. 'I want you. And as soon as possible.' I looked at my glass, because I was ashamed to look at her. 'God knows, I've take long enough about making up my mind. But now I have, I'm in a hurry.' I felt as if tears were going to come into my eyes. 'I want to make up for lost time. You know that, don't you, darling?'

Myrtle nodded lovingly, without a sign of reproach.

We were silent. The room was filled with loud polyglottal talk, yet we might have been alone.

'I wish you'd write and tell him!' I said.

'Darling...' We had already discussed the topic at great length.

'I know,' I said. 'But can't you change your mind?'

'It isn't a question of changing my mind. I just couldn't do it, darling. We've got to wait until he comes home. I shall have to see him, to tell him.'

I said: 'I should have thought it would be easier to write a letter than to say it.'

'Then you don't understand,' Myrtle said bitterly. 'It's easier for you than for me.'

I said: 'I can't say I feel so wonderful about it. Making love to his wife while he's overseas. And then asking him to give us a divorce when he comes home.'

'He thinks you're a cad, anyway.'

'Well, really!' I felt cross, outraged.

Myrtle stared round the room.

'If that's so,' I said, 'at least it won't come as a surprise.'

Myrtle turned slowly back to me. 'I had a long letter from him this morning. He doesn't know there's anything the matter.'

It seemed to me incredible. Myrtle wrote to him regularly. I said nothing.

'He thinks,' she said, 'he may be sent to Palestine.'

'Further away,' said I.

Myrtle ignored my remark. She said:

'I suppose it's dangerous, isn't it?'

'Dangerous?'

'Yes,' Myrtle said, impatiently. 'I suppose there are ambushes, and all that.'

'I suppose so.'

Myrtle had a sad, thoughtful, apprehensive expression, while she considered ambushes.

I did not speak, because, watching Myrtle's face, it came to me that though she could not face without great pain the prospect of wounding Haxby by asking for a divorce, she could face with just a shade less pain the prospect of his being eliminated by the Stern Gang. Poor Haxby!

Myrtle was silent for quite a long time. Then she said: 'I suppose we ought to go home.'

'Julia asked us not to.'

Myrtle glanced at me sideways. Her eyelids flickered.

'Don't you remember, darling?' I said.

Myrtle smiled, in a sly deprecating way that was next door to accusation.

At that moment a fresh contingent of guests arrived. We were surprised. The party suddenly came to life again. Through the crowd I tried to catch Julia's eye, but it was impossible. We decided to make our way across the room to join the party surrounding the minister and the general.

Robert looked pleased to see us. The trouble about attaching oneself to the most distinguished guests at a party is that it is not very easy to leave them.

Julia drew me close to her. She said in my ear:

'I must have a moment with you. *Tête-à-tête*. I'm going to take you to the buffet.'

I was puzzled. She was in high spirits, gay, excited and drunk.

'Robert's had a wild success,' she said. 'He's been invited to visit Warsaw.'

I thought Robert's chances were remote, since I gathered all the Poles present were strongly anti-Communist.

'Fantastic idea,' I said.

'Fantastic people,' Julia whispered.

We reached the buffet and Julia held an animated discussion with a waiter.

'What are you asking him for?' I said.

'Some things like little *vol-au-vents* made with shrimps.' She put her hand on my arm. 'While you're waiting try one of those slices of cucumber with honey on it. Robert says you like food.'

'Wonderful girl!' Out of enthusiasm I patted her, below the level of the table. It seemed she was wearing nothing under her dress. She turned on me and said:

'Now we're going across to the bar.'

We went to the bar, and she asked for drinks. She had somehow communicated an extraordinary tension to me. I felt as if we were in a heady kind of dream. We were looking at each other. Her eyes bulged at me with a winking brightness.

'Well?' I said.

'I don't know how to begin.' She glanced round, furtively, with her head bent.

'All right. I'll wait. . .'

We looked at each other again, and suddenly a startling exchange of remarks took place.

Fixing me with her winking brightness of eye, Julia said in amused, penetrating and ironic, friendly detachment: 'There's something slightly feminine about you.'

And instantly I said, in just the same way: 'And there's something slightly masculine about you.'

No offence was either meant or taken, on either side. We just stared at each other, amused and surprised.

'Is that what you wanted to tell me?' I said.

Julia shook her head. 'Oh no!' Her hair swung softly.

I thought we must both be drunk. I said:

'What on earth was it?'

She glanced round urgently.

'Here come Robert and Myrtle. I shall have to tell you now.' She suddenly took hold of my hand. 'You mustn't tell anyone.' She leaned towards me, so that her lips almost touched my ear. *'I'm not really married to Wladislaw!'*

CHAPTER III

MORNING BEFORE THE OFFICE

Robert and I had adjoining offices and we always met first thing in the morning for exchange of private news. The one who arrived first went through his correspondence perfunctorily, waiting for the face of the other to come round the door. And what a face he often saw!

'What's happened *now*?'

That was the tone of the first question, and it was usually justified. Sometimes one of us would silently hand over a letter. At present I am telling you about only Robert and myself: we had numerous intimate friends, in whose lives we were bound up – so that when no blow of fate was striking us we could expect it to be striking one of them.

On the morning after the Anglo-Polish party I arrived at the office first. For some little time it had been usual for me to arrive first. Robert, in his fine sombre hat and his coat that made him look like a Minister of the Crown, was arriving later and later in the day. And when he did arrive he was showing signs of not getting home till earlier and earlier in the morning – a hot brightness of the eye, a crookedness of the parting, a greyness of the cheek.

Robert came into the office. It was about half-past ten on a late autumnal morning, the sort of dully-lit morning when it seemed as if a trace of fog had got into the room. He smoothed his hair and sat on the corner of my desk. I laid aside a secret memorandum from the Ministry of Defence, and said:

'You don't look as if you've had much sleep, old boy.'

Robert picked up the memorandum instead of meeting my eye. 'Four hours.' He put it down again. There was a pause. The pause was dramatic. He said:

'Julia's told me what she told you last night.'

This left me temporarily with nothing to say.

'What did you think of it?' he said.

'I wanted to know the rest of the story.'

'I can tell you that.' He glanced at me. 'I'll tell it you as it was told to me. Though in a rather more coherent form.'

I pushed my chair back, and put up my feet on the edge of an open drawer while I listened.

'Her story is that Wladislaw was passionately anxious to marry her and that she didn't want to. In fact, she refused to marry him. Certain other things she didn't refuse. They were living together. So she agreed to compromise by changing her name to Mrs Łempicki-Czyz by deed-poll.'

'She must be crazy.'

'You must judge that for yourself.'

'Was Czyz already married?'

'There you show more insight. Yes. He was already married, but he insisted that his wife was killed by the Germans shortly after he escaped from Poland. In his opinion it was perfectly reasonable for Julia to marry him. And if not reasonable, perfectly legal. It appears that he explained this to her very clearly, and at great length. He was very anxious to marry her. I don't blame him.'

'Didn't she believe his wife was dead?'

'She couldn't be sure. One of her friends married a Czech, whose wife turned up in England about six months later. It seems to have shaken Julia's faith in Wladislaw, though I don't see why it should.'

'Does he still want to marry her?'

'Yes. He's gone back to Poland to prove that his wife is dead. He's convinced that if he brings back suitable evidence, Julia's objections will be overcome.'

'When he comes back he'll expect her to marry him.' I suddenly wondered if Robert was going to marry her before Wladislaw appeared.

'He's always expecting her to marry him.'

'But she wants you to marry her.'

'I suspect that's why she sent him back to Poland.'

I felt slightly dizzy.

Robert was watching me, enjoying my incomprehension.

'You insist on concentrating on what happens when people come back,' he said. 'Everyone else concentrates on what happens while they're still away.'

I thought he was criticising Myrtle. Before I could reply the telephone rang. I said I was in conference with Robert.

Robert had got up and strolled across the room. He was looking at a set of German ordnance maps that I had fastened to the wall with drawing-pins. I was not interested in the topography of Germany: I kept them as souvenirs, and I liked to see the brilliant blue patches of lake and sea shining from my dirty cream-painted walls.

'They don't extend to Poland,' Robert observed. As I put down the receiver he returned and drew up a chair beside me. He lit a cigarette.

'People get themselves into fantastic situations,' he said. He had dropped his tone of bantering amusement. 'We've seen a lot, old boy. But we've still got a lot to learn.' He grinned. 'And I suspect we've still got a good many surprises coming to us.'

We were both thinking about Julia. Robert said solemnly:

'It was an extraordinary experience. To have this history interspersed with incidents of a different kind.'

'There's no nicer place to listen to a woman's life-story than in bed.'

I had overstepped the mark of Robert's taste. He thoughtfully adjusted the position of his cigarette in its holder. He said:

'I don't know the whole story of her and Wladislaw. But it's obvious that he made a deep impression on her. I'm sure that in slightly different circumstances she would have married him. She's had numerous offers since she went to live with him. Offers of marriage. And turned them down.'

'Until you.'

'Until me.'

We were silent.

'She's a very remarkable girl.'

It was the same phrase again. He made it in a tone of deep feeling, and it seemed to express all the fascination, all the drawing-together of two different souls. I glanced at him. I knew that however much he loved her he would never say it in so many words. 'Very remarkable,' he repeated.

I said: 'All this means that you can marry her. She's free.'

We were silent. Suddenly I was aware that the atmosphere had changed. I was surprised. Robert was looking at me in a way I did not understand.

'In some ways you're the most worldly of men, Joe. In others you're extraordinarily innocent.'

Instantly I knew what he was going to say. I could have blushed.

'She's free,' said Robert, 'if all this happens to be the truth.'

CHAPTER IV

A NEW COLLEAGUE

When members of our staff came into the office in the morning and found Robert and me deep in discussion, at least some of them must have presumed that we were deciding the policy of our division. In offices throughout the government service, all over the country, bosses and their assistants were conferring on policy before the day's work began.

Robert had made up his mind on our policy over the A 15 long ago. Morning before the office was reserved for other purposes. One bright October morning Dr R. A. Chubb arrived, and his ideas were entirely different from ours. He was waiting in Robert's office, ready to discuss policy, before Robert arrived.

Robert promptly came to fetch me.

'How did *he* get in?' he whispered.

I shook my head, and followed him back to his office.

Dr Chubb was standing between Robert's desk and the window.

'I was just admiring the view,' he said. 'It's a very good office you have here.' He turned to Robert with the speculative air of a man who is wondering what sort of an office is going to be assigned to him and is presuming that it will be no less good.

As Robert proposed to send Chubb away immediately on a tour of firms, he had arranged for him temporarily to share my office. From Robert's window you could look into the corner of Parliament Square; from mine you could have looked into the well of the building if anyone had seen fit to remove the material pasted over it to prevent splintering in air-raids.

I looked at Dr Chubb while Robert was breaking the news to him. I judged him to be about fifty-eight. He was comfortably built, not as tall as Robert, and neatly dressed in a blue suit.

At first sight Dr Clubb would never be mistaken for a deep and powerful thinker. His bulging wide-open blue eyes had a faint look of alarm in them, and so had his mouth, which always seemed to be nervously showing his front teeth. His expression was amiable, not particularly constrained in spite of his air of alarm, and mildly absurd. Its absurdity was enhanced by a touch of old-womanishness – he wore reading spectacles that consisted of only the lower halves of lenses and he looked over the top of them all the time.

'I've been having a look at the accommodation this morning,' Dr Chubb was saying, hare-eyedly and toothily to Robert.

I thought he had not taken long about it. I looked at him with more interest. His rosy face was that of a man whom I would have expected to be dim by ordinary standards of the government service. Physically he was middle-aged and tamed. And yet I was not surprised that he was quite capable of looking after himself. Dim, yes. And shrewd. And probably persistent, too.

Robert was treating Dr Chubb with lofty consideration. He adumbrated his plan for sending Dr Chubb on tour as if he were conferrrng a great privilege upon him and at the same time giving him the opportunity to win the unfading gratitude of his country.

'In view of my expectation that you'd ask me to undertake this matter,' Dr Chubb began, in a humble, nervous, unhurried style, 'I gave it a certain amount of thought, as a consequence of which I concluded that I should like to make a few suggestions myself.' He paused. 'I fully realise the urgency of what you're asking me to do, but I think you'll probably agree with me that sometimes – especially on occasions like this – it doesn't do to be too hasty.' He stopped, looking as if he were expecting congratulation.

Robert stared at him.

'In the course of thinking it over,' Dr Chubb went on, 'it

occurred to me that there were one or two proposals, certainly one proposal, which I should like to put before you for your consideration. Personally I think it is worth considering myself, that we should try and take advantage' – he paused – 'of every offer of help we can get, especially from all those, if you understand what I mean, who are in a position to help us.'

'Quite,' said Robert, with a mixture of decision and patience that I could only hope to emulate.

Dr Chubb pursued his course in his own tempo.

I was attentive enough to realise the important phrase was 'all those who can help us'. Dr Chubb's proposal, when he finally came to it, was that we should go for 'help' to the federation of owners of the industries. He wound up with an open-eyed solemn expression.

'I naturally don't want to influence whatever plans you have in mind one way or the other, but I'm convinced that we can't do better than put ourselves in their hands, in order to form for ourselves a really comprehensive view of the position.'

Robert received the proposal thoughtfully.

Rules about security impose on me the disadvantage of not being able to tell you what the industries were: they now as a consequence enable me to tell you, with delightful freedom from fear of libel, that I personally thought half the owners were sharks and the federation next door to a racket.

'I think it's an excellent proposal,' said Robert, catching Dr Chubb's solemnity. 'If this survey is to be as valuable as we all think it's going to be, it's most important that we should carry the industries with us.'

Dr Chubb appeared to bloom with pleasure.

'I should like to say that it so happens,' he said, 'that I know Lord —— personally.' He named the president of the federation. 'I knew him when he was Sir —— ——.'

'Ah!' said Robert, cutting short personal reminiscence of a historical nature.

My own first impulse would have been to reject the proposal. Put ourselves in *their* hands, indeed! Now I saw what Robert was up to.

'I didn't anticipate approaching Lord —— in the first place,' Dr Chubb went on. 'He's a very busy man – '

'I think I can do that,' Robert interrupted. 'I meet him frequently on committee.'

Dr Chubb was momentarily deflated, but he picked up. 'It's possible you may think differently, if he's a close colleague of yours, but I should doubt myself if we should need him in the initial stages.' He could not prevent the return of a faintly self-satisfied air. 'I should like to say also that the secretary of the federation is an old friend of mine.' He quietly rolled off the name of another gentleman who had been knighted for services to industry. There was a peculiar look on Dr Chubb's face whenever he said Lord or Sir, a look of mingled reverence, delight and aspiration.

'Ah,' Robert said again. He glanced at me.

'And there's Sir Harold Deemer,' Dr Chubb went on, never apparently having had enough.

'And Sir Joseph Floyd,' said Robert.

'I think,' said Dr Chubb, 'there's every indication of our being able to make a thorough job of it.' And his tone of voice gave the show away completely: he was hoping for some kind of honour for himself.

'I have great hopes,' Robert said, encouraging him. He was now waiting for Dr Chubb to go.

Dr Chubb had no thoughts of going. He said: 'Sometime before I start out, I should like to have a talk with you. About the policy you would like me to pursue.'

'Certainly,' said Robert. 'Let us talk about it now.'

'I am, of course, entirely at your disposal. It is entirely for you to lay down the manner in which you wish the survey to be conducted.'

For a moment, I was puzzled. Then I saw Dr Chubb's aim. Having shown that he was bringing inestimable connections to our division, he had to assure us that the connections were not in any way binding.

'I know that my own department has tended to make up its mind already,' Dr Chubb said. 'But I shouldn't like you to think that I have.' He looked at Robert with a kind of diffident confidence. 'I wouldn't have accepted this post if it had been otherwise.' He hesitated. 'I don't like this controversy over the A 15 and the A 16, and I feel it's a great pity that it arose as it did.'

Robert made a gesture, as much as to say that these things happen. He was looking interestedly at Dr Chubb. He must have been wondering, just as I was wondering, exactly to what extent Dr Chubb was speaking the truth. I had assumed, in a superficially cynical way, that Dr Chubb had been sent to us to further the policy of his own department. When I heard him speak I was not entirely sure.

'I don't want it to be thought,' Dr Chubb went on, 'by anyone, that I accepted this post for reasons that were in any way improper, because I know the function of D.O.R.R.S. is to be impartial, and I think I may truthfully say that I'm impartial myself, so impartial that I am coming' – he paused – 'to this post with a completely open mind.'

'I'm sure of that,' said Robert. It was a formal remark, but the tone was cordial. I did not understand it.

'I have assured Sir Francis Plumer to that effect.'

Robert nodded.

From this point they went on to discuss matters of detail at great length. I had heard it all before. I was concentrating on the conversation I have recorded. I kept asking myself a question to which I could not find the answer. Who, I wanted to know, was taking in whom?

CHAPTER V

A YELLOW SAPPHIRE

At this time Myrtle used always to pause, when we were walking down Bond Street, before the window of a jeweller's shop. She had her eye on a sapphire ring. The stone was an exquisite yellow and beautifully cut: it was like a small transparent box filled with pure limpid sunlight.

The price of the ring was seven hundred pounds, and let me say at once that I had no intention of buying it. As our marriage drew nearer I felt less and less like the greatest writer since Shakespeare and more and more like a poor government official.

'I must go and look at my ring,' Myrtle used to say, whenever we were nearby. The shop was only small, but it was in the narrowest part of the street and there was no missing it. I acquiesced. Only a woman, I thought, could call 'my' something she was never likely to possess.

Myrtle sighed as she stared at the ring. I watched her. Then Myrtle glanced at me, and I had to admit the possibility of seeing in a woman's eyes, even in the eyes of the woman one loves, a light of frank cupidity.

'It's lovely,' I said. 'How vulgar the diamonds look beside it!' The diamonds cost anything up to three thousand pounds and there were a lot of them in the window.

'I like the diamonds, too,' said Myrtle. 'A girl never says no to diamonds.'

'Sometimes the man who's got to pay for them does.'

'Darling!' Myrtle laid her hand on my arm, and looked up at me lovingly. 'I don't expect you to buy it me.'

I thought I must be heartless and crude, with even a touch of the mercenary. 'I know,' I said. 'Darling.'

On the other hand I sometimes had intimations of the boot being on the other foot. Whenever Robert was with us, we stopped just the same, but the conversation took another tone.

'There you are, old boy,' Robert would say, as we looked at the yellow sapphire. 'There you are' – in a hearty cynical voice. 'That's what you've got to work for.'

And Myrtle would look up at him with an appreciative, conspiratorial smirk.

Myrtle would have liked me to give her the ring. Of course she would. Yet she was no more heartless nor mercenary than I. The ring had somehow become a symbol to her. If I gave her the yellow sapphire it would show how much I loved her. The fact that it would show literally – that I loved her to the tune of seven hundred pounds – was secondary though highly desirable. I thought of how many women I had known who loved presents for this reason. Presents as a proof of being loved – I was touched by the simplicity of it. Would they never realise some men's pockets were more easily touched than their hearts?

Myrtle's playful covetousness persisted longer than I expected. And then one day I realised the yellow sapphire had somehow become the focus of a conflict. We were strolling along Bond Street after lunch. It was near the end of November, and the weather was cold and drizzly. I remember it very well because Myrtle had an umbrella which I was holding over her head. The umbrella was made of tartan silk, with a fair amount of red in it, and although the light was grey it cast a coloured glow on Myrtle's cheeks. The road was glossy with moisture, and the tyres of silent expensive cars made a creaking noise on it as they passed.

'I must look at my ring, darling.' Myrtle was cheerful. She had her arm linked in mine. As she stopped before the window, I swung round, keeping the umbrella over her. We looked at the ring.

Myrtle sighed. 'There it is.' She glanced at me thoughtfully. 'I suppose we shall both be too old to want it by the time we can afford it.'

'Depends on how much money we make.'

'Oh, you'll make a lot, darling.'

'So will you, sweet.' I tried to slip the remark in easily. I had not looked forward to the first time this subject appeared in our discussions.

'Me?' she said. 'I'm not going to go on working after we're married.'

'Why not?'

'You've got to keep me, my lad.'

'Oh!' I was not surprised by her firm rejection of my plan, but felt compelled not to give it up.

'You don't sound enthusiastic, darling.'

'What man's ever been enthusiastic about doubling his cost of living without doubling his income?' I said.

Myrtle glanced at me, and it was clear that she found the remark neither true nor funny, let alone both.

'I should have thought you'd have wanted to keep me,' she said.

'And lose a thousand sweet smackers per annum?' I said, trying to keep the tone of the conversation light.

Myrtle said: 'Sometimes I don't understand you at all, darling.' The conversation was not light. Her tone was of grave reproach. We both knew it was a serious moment.

Myrtle and I stared at each other, under the brightly coloured umbrella. The drizzle fell around us. The yellow sapphire glittered from the window. People jostled against us on the pavement. We stared because we were two different persons, different in temperament, different in desires, confronting each other, each impelled by self.

I drew Myrtle round, away from the window, and said:

'Let's move on, darling.'

We walked side by side, in step. Neither of us said anything till we came to a street corner, where we had to wait for the traffic before we could cross.

'I really don't understand you, darling.'

Myrtle's tone had lost its reproach, but from its determination I knew that she did not want to let the discussion drop.

'It's quite simple,' I said.

'Is it? It doesn't seem simple to me.'

'What? The concept of a thousand pounds a year?'

'I didn't mean that.'

'But I did. We won't have a lot of money when we're married. A thousand a year will make a lot of difference.' I glanced at her. 'I want us to live in style and comfort, darling.'

'But I don't want to go on working.'

'Why not?'

Myrtle looked down for a moment, and then she said: 'Most husbands keep their wives, don't they?'

For an instant I was tempted to say 'Yours doesn't'. Haxby's pre-war income was about half Myrtle's, and he had lived in her father's house. Instead I said:

'Most wives aren't talented enough to earn a thousand a year.' I spoke the last phrase as warmly as I could.

Myrtle was irritated and embarrassed. We were still standing in the same place on the street corner. The flow of traffic had ceased, but she made no attempt to cross the road. She said with great feeling:

'Why can't you be like other men?'

I too was brought to a standstill. The times I had asked myself the same question – and not, as people always imagined, in a tone of self-concerned, narcissistic moral rectitude. How many times had I asked it in alarm, in bewilderment, and even in misery. I was old enough now to think that I had a singular temperament. Ninety-nine men out of a hundred perfectly naturally wanted to keep their wives. Myrtle was right. In this part of her nature she was a very ordinary young woman. It was I who could not fit into the ordinary pattern of life.

'Because I'm not made like other men.'

Myrtle looked at me, and I could tell she found it a remark of incomprehensible peevish arrogance. She was too hurt and angry to reply.

'When we're married I want you to keep some independence,' I said, trying to get somewhere near to explaining my feelings. What could I say, when I had never understood them clearly myself? I thought it was some kind of responsibility for her that I wanted to evade. But I knew that in the end it was the abandonment of myself to the complete intimacy of marriage that I resisted: I wanted to hold Myrtle off, and making her have a career of her own seemed to me at the time a way of doing it. It was irrational, peculiar, and, I suppose crazy.

'But what if I don't want independence?' said Myrtle, just as any man but me might have expected.

'Then try to want it for my sake,' I cried.

'Why?'

'Because I want to keep some independence of my own.' I suddenly burst out: 'I don't want to feel the chains!'

'Darling?' My outbursts in metaphor always left her stupefied.

I glanced at her. I tried to smile.

'I'm not going to interfere with your independence.' Myrtle spoke as if such a thing were impossible. She paused. Drizzle fell outside the edge of the umbrella. Her face, lit by the patches of tartan glow, was suddenly gentle and kind.

'What's my salary beside yours, darling?' she asked. 'Beside what you *can* earn.'

'What I *can* earn? How?'

'By writing. You can make thousands, darling. I'm sure of it.'

I forgot the disadvantages of a singular temperament in sheer surprise. My novels up to date had been well-received but had shown no signs of bringing in more than a few hundred pounds between them. And as works of art, they had made the smallest of impressions on Myrtle anyway – even out of her great love for me she never pretended to the contrary.

'Robert thinks so, too,' Myrtle said.

'You've been talking to him about it!'

'He's sure you can make a lot of money.'

'How? If I can, why haven't I?'

'If you'll write the sort of things people like, darling.'

With this classic wifely remark, Myrtle had the effrontery to lean affectionately closer to me.

People were passing us all the while. Their umbrellas caught against mine. I was aware of nothing but the proposition Myrtle was shrewdly and lovingly putting to me, the proposition that I should sell myself.

'If you'll write things that are just funny,' Myrtle said,

'people will love it.'

I saw now why during the last few weeks Myrtle had brought me a series of books by successful humorists.

'Now I know!' I cried. 'Now I know what you want. You don't just want a sapphire ring. You don't just want me to keep you. You want everything. Literally, *everything!*'

'Oh!' The smile vanished from Myrtle's lips, and the whites of her eyes reddened and shone with tears.

'Darling,' I said. I lowered the umbrella and kissed her.

'You don't understand me,' she said. The tears went back again, and she gave me a tremulous melancholy smile. I had to be gentle with her.

'We don't understand each other, if you ask me.'

We paused. I have no doubt that you understand us only too well. It is always easy to perceive the moral defects of someone else.

Myrtle said: 'Don't you think we ought to walk on?'

I glanced at my watch. 'Good God, yes.'

The traffic was moving steadily past, so we had to wait again. I noticed two women talking under an umbrella beside us, enormously big girls with French accents, mink stoles, and very fancy shoes. They were prostitutes from Cork Street. Myrtle was silent. Suddenly she touched my hand and said:

'I'm willing to go on working for the first three years.'

'Darling!' I turned to her with relief. 'A compromise!' Nothing could be more in tune with my ideas than a compromise. I had a tiresome temperament, but I was willing to try and cope with it if Myrtle would meet me half way. I thought five years would have been more satisfactory, but I did not care to argue. Myrtle had seen sense.

The traffic suddenly paused: there was an opening before us and we crossed the road at last. I had my arm round Myrtle's waist. She leaned against me as we walked along. She appeared to be glancing in shop-windows. I did the same. I saw some handsome shirts and ties, a beautiful painting of a canal by Boudin, the posters of a theatre-ticket agency. The drizzle had ceased. I suddenly felt convinced that given time and gradualness the selfish claims of my temperament might break and our marriage be a success.

At Piccadilly we had to part. I shut the umbrella, and stood facing Myrtle, waiting to see what she would say to feed my heart with hope.

Myrtle sighed, carelessly and comfortably. Then she said: 'Ah, well ... I suppose I shall start having a baby straight away.'

CHAPTER VI
NOTE ON ART

Though I had not written anything for seven years, because of the war, my art, I should like you to understand, was very important to me. Myrtle and I argued over it regularly. In this context my art was nothing abstract: it was the novels I intended to write. Myrtle, Robert, all my friends, had strong views on what sort of novels they ought to be. Their views, I hardly need say, they propounded for my own good, so it was no wonder we nearly came to blows over them.

Just as Robert and I were different as men, so were we different as writers. What we both wanted to do was more or less the same: the way we were going to try and do it was appropriate to our temperaments. Robert proposed to achieve his end through a kind of romantic and dramatic power, I through a kind of humour and wit. Naturally I thought I had some power, and Robert flagrantly fancied his chance as a wag. I was willing, being a fair-minded man, to admit that Robert did sometimes overlap my terrain – he was definitely funny. Robert, on the other hand, yielded me not a square inch of his territory.

You may say that our arguments at this point were academic. Just so. But may I remind you that Robert and I were working for the day when we might throw off the shackles of His Majesty's service and emerge free artists at last? It was essential that we should decide what kind of books we were going to write, because free artists can only pursue their beautiful high ideals if they previously take the precaution of selling their works for some money.

Robert was a part-time civil servant, I was a temporary one – we could break the links at any moment. The moment had got to come. Soon. And what then?

'If you'll only write things that are just funny, darling, people will love it.'

Just funny! Those two words. Red rag to a bull.

I tried to explain to Myrtle that I could only imagine a novel being funny about something. To ask for a novel to be just funny was like asking for the smile off the Cheshire cat – which was of course just what Myrtle wanted. I sought a more concrete image. I said:

'It's like asking you to make a woman's hat that's purely decorative – and doesn't cover her head.'

'Women's hats don't cover their heads,' said Myrtle.

Back to the abstract. Myrtle conceded that I had got to be funny about something. I said, in my novels, the something must be the stuff of human experience; and at least half the stuff of human experience is misery, torment and disaster.

'Don't write about that half,' said Myrtle promptly.

'It wouldn't be the truth if I missed it out. I must write about it.'

I hope you follow me. Many did not. Myrtle said impatiently:

'But darling, it can't be funny if you put it in.'

'Why not?'

Myrtle gave me a look of frank astonishment.

'Why not?' I repeated.

Myrtle had ceased to follow me at all. I retired into my thoughts, where I could still have my way. I recalled the words of a greater writer than myself, Horace, who had asked in powerful entreaty, 'Why should one not speak the truth, laughing?' That was what I wanted to do – it was not a question of being funny or not being funny. *To speak the truth, laughing*! How I knew what he must have felt like, how my heart went out to him! It was the last word, the most perfect word, on his art and on mine. Inflated, inspired, I said to Myrtle:

'I want to speak the truth, laughing. I'll do it or I'll die in the attempt!'

Myrtle looked at me as if she thought I was mad.

CHAPTER VII

CALLING LATE AT NIGHT

I was reading alone in my flat when the bell rang that called me to the telephone. I was surprised. The time was nearly midnight. There was only one telephone, in the hall near the front door. As I ran downstairs I met the landlady coming up in her dressing-gown.

'You're wanted on the telephone.' Her journey upstairs was quite unnecessary. I stared at her.

'It's a woman,' she said. I realised I was wrong. Her journey had been undertaken from the over-riding necessity of expressing moral disapproval.

'Excellent,' I said, not attempting to conceal my satisfaction at observing that moral disapproval made her face look even meaner and even more ladylike than it was before. I had no idea who the woman was.

As I ran along the hall to the telephone, the landlady bustled into her flat at the end of the corridor and left the door ajar to facilitate eavesdropping on my conversation.

It was Julia.

'I want you to come and see me, Joe. Now.' She stopped, agitatedly. 'Don't think I'm mad.'

'I'll reserve my judgment on that.'

'Will you come?'

'Yes.'

I put down the receiver and ran upstairs for my overcoat. My landlady must have reached an insomniaic pitch of distraction on hearing me close the front door behind me.

It happened that Julia lived in a big block of flats less than half a mile along the Embankment from my house. I had often debated with Robert the project of paying her a neighbourly call.

'She'll think you want to sleep with her,' he would reply, with unusual simplicity and directness. 'That's all.'

So I gave up the project. And I recalled Robert's words as I made my way rapidly along the Embankment and heard Big Ben chiming behind me. It was a cold windy night. I turned up the collar on my overcoat and pulled my hat over my eyes. As I passed a square with trees in it a gust of dry, frozen leaves blew round my heels.

A porter showed me the right entrance and I went up in the lift to Julia's flat. It was on the eighth floor, at the end of a stuffy internal corridor.

Julia opened the door, and I looked into rooms that were close-carpeted and all painted pale green. It was like being inside a set of inter-communicating match-boxes. One felt enclosed and remote, either very high up in the air or possibly below the sea.

'This is my end of the flat.' Julia shared it with another girl. 'There's nobody else in.' She walked ahead of me, wearing a frock of dark red silk that rustled. Through the bathroom door I saw a pink slip and some silk stockings drying on a chromium towel-rail. There was a smell of scent and something else.

In the room Julia turned and faced me. I knew what she was going to say.

'I'm drinking brandy.'

That is what the other smell was, the sweet clinging spirituous odour of brandy.

'So I see.' There was a glass and a bottle on a low table beside the sofa. I glanced round the room. It was softly lit, rather over-heated, and somewhat untidy. There was a satinwood writing-table, a grand piano with some silver-framed photographs on it, dark brocade curtains, and no flowers anywhere.

'You must drink some brandy.' Julia was looking at me with a strained nervous smile. Her chin was lowered and her bright grey eyes seemed to be bulging at me. There were some specks of powder on the front of her dress. She was slightly drunk.

I took off my overcoat and sat down. She gave me a glass. It was good brandy. After a few preliminary hiccups I began to drink it steadily with pleasure. There was a lot of it.

Julia moved from one place to another in the room. Suddenly she stopped and said:

'Where's Robert?'

'I don't know.'

'I thought you wouldn't.'

I was puzzled. 'Why not?'

'He was supposed to be here tonight.'

I thought she must be drunker than she looked.

Julia said: 'He didn't come. So I settled down with the brandy bottle.' She pointed to it. 'The bottle was full at seven o'clock.'

I said: 'I'm sure he hasn't done it on purpose. Are you sure you've not got the wrong night yourself?'

Julia did not reply. She shook her hair back from her face, and came rapidly towards my chair. I must confess I thought it was me she was making for – it turned out to be the telephone, which stood on a little table beside me. Julia sat on the arm of my chair, and swiftly dialled Robert's number.

'Listen!' she said, waving the receiver in the air. There was no reply.

'I really don't know where he is,' I said. 'Keep calm.'

Julia put the receiver down, and remained where she was. She turned to look at me, and her breast was very close to my cheek.

'You shouldn't take to the bottle so easily,' I said.

I thought her voice changed, and that she leaned a little closer. 'I might do worse.'

I looked up, and saw her eyes, her breast.

She whispered: 'I could, you know.'

I did not doubt it. And if it comes to that, I was far from certain of myself.

'Yes,' I said, forcing my head not to budge.

'I've been faithful to Robert for six weeks.'

I moved my head back, in order to drink some brandy. I drank a lot. 'That's not long,' I said.

'It is for me.' She stood up. 'I'm trying!' she cried. 'Because I love him!'

The remark was wrung from her. Moved by it, I jumped to

my feet.

'I've never done it for anyone else,' she said.

We were facing each other, looking into each other's eyes. She said to me: 'And I've had a lot of men.'

I said to her: 'You must be terribly unhappy.'

Immediately she burst into laughter. 'I liked it!'

And at this moment the effects of the brandy struck me. The pale green walls seemed to fall back into space. She swayed towards me. I thought 'My God!'

I tensed the whole of my body.

'Robert and I,' I heard myself saying, as if it were someone else, 'never share a woman.'

I thought 'He's done it!' – he being I – with a burst of emotion that was either strong approval or strong disapproval, I did not know which.

'You've just left Myrtle,' she said.

I addressed her with deep intentness. 'We never share a woman. Or a publisher.'

I can still remember the gleam of drunken mystification in her eye. This did not weaken my determination to complete what seemed like a profound statement of truth.

'I won't have jealousy,' I said. I spoke slowly but not coherently. 'You can change your woman. You can change your publisher. But you can't change your friends.' I, myself, was not quite sure how publishers had got into the argument. I ended up solemnly.

'Friends take a long time to make.'

Julia was looking at me with a bright stare.

'I've no idea what you're talking about,' she said, in a slightly edgy tone. 'But I grasp the intention.'

'Oh,' I said, non-committally.

'I suppose some men say No.'

'I don't know about that. I can tell you that quite a few women do.'

'I can't understand it!'

'Quite a few don't, fortunately.'

'I can't understand how any woman can say No!' Julia spoke with force.

I laughed. Then I thought again. I said:

'You must be unhappy.'

'I'm not!' She was furious. She suddenly raised her arm as if she were going to throw the contents of her glass at me. 'You prig! You say No to me and then tell me I'm unhappy.'

I felt myself sway. 'Good God, that brandy's hit me between wind and water.'

Julia put out her hand to steady me. She grinned and furtively glanced downward.

'You'd better have some more.'

She poured out another glass. I sat down. Julia sat on the arm of my chair again. A fold of her dark red silk dress fell across my lap. Her mood changed. Suddenly she said:

'I suppose you don't think much of me.'

'I don't think much of myself.'

She glanced at me thoughtfully: 'I suppose you don't.'

'Don't imagine that I think much of anybody else either!'

Julia said: 'You ought to think more of yourself.'

I laughed. 'Thanks for the advice.' I drank some more brandy. The room was very quiet. There was no sound from the hundreds of flats around us. I could hear Julia breathing. She took hold of a tuft of my hair and began to twist it.

'I wish Robert were here,' she said.

'I'm Joe. Get it straight. I'm drunk but still Joe.'

'Where's Robert?'

'You've asked that before.'

She seized the telephone again.

'Don't do that!' I said.

'Why not?' She paused to glance at me.

'You won't do yourself any good.'

'I don't care.'

I took hold of her hand and dragged it away from the dial.

'I won't sit down under it!' she cried. Her fingers tightened on mine.

'That's no reason for promptly getting on to your back.'

'Isn't it?' She was startled. Then suddenly her laughter burst out again, high-pitched, constrained, and yet gleeful.

We looked into each other's eyes, and I am sure we were drawn together in some kind of deep emotion.

'What's wrong with me?' she said. The question sprang

right up, and I could see her anxiety to know the answer shining nakedly in her face. She waited.

I held her hand. 'You're off the rails, my dear.'

'What's the use of saying that?' she cried: 'I know. I know!'

'It's never much use saying anything, but you asked me.'

She stood up. She ran her hand through her soft silky hair: it fell beautifully back into place. 'Why am I off the rails?' She was looking away.

I was drunk and I could not help myself from saying what was in my heart. 'Because you've got no sense. Because you don't know what you want. Because you keep on doing something when you ought to do nothing.'

'I know what I want.' She turned to me.

I did not speak.

'And I suppose you call it "doing something when I ought to do nothing" when I refuse to sit down under things.'

I still did not speak.

'I know what I want.' Her voice was raised.

'What?' I asked mildly.

'I want Robert to marry me.'

'Yes.'

'Don't you see? I'm in love with him. He's the most wonderful man I ever met.' She spoke passionately and then suddenly changed her tone. 'He's the one man for me. He's older than me. He's – I don't know . . . He can master me. He can be a father as well as a lover!' She stopped as if the inspiration had only just come to her. 'That's what he is,' she said, and her eyes widened. 'It's what I want. It's what I need.' She looked at me. 'He can bring me back on to the rails, and keep me there. When we're married, all this' – she made a gesture with her hand – 'will come to an end. And I shall be really happy.' The last sentence lay vibrant on the warm still air. Then she turned to me. 'I suppose you think I'm a fool!'

'No. I don't think you're a fool.'

'What do you think I am?'

I could not speak. In a flash the words had run through my mind – 'You're a lost soul'. And I could not say them. I saw her standing before me, strong and active, beautiful, and wild with conflict.

'What?' she cried again.

I was deeply moved. I shook my head. I said softly: 'I don't know.'

Julia lit a cigarette. I sipped a little brandy, and began to take in details of the room mechanically. Dust on the keys of the piano, ostrich plumes in the hair of one of the women in the photographs, the heels of a pair of bronze kid shoes peeping from under the sofa. I felt a new thought stirring.

Julia said: 'Do you think Robert will marry me?'

She might have known what I was thinking. I had indeed begun to see how she might take hold of Robert's imagination, and I could momentarily feel only distress. It was in Robert's temperament to be deeply drawn to lost souls. The Headlamps, frigid and beautiful, tormenting and tormented, was another, different, lost soul. And I knew that those things which drew him on to begin with could only make him wretched in the end. Had Julia asked me, 'Do you think Robert will love me?' I should have had to answer against my will: 'He may. He may ...'

'Will he marry you!' I began, not knowing what to say.

There was a noise in the corridor outside.

'It's my room-mate coming in,' said Julia. 'Go on.'

I glanced at the door, which was open, hesitating as if I did not want to be overheard.

'It's all right,' Julia said impatiently.

To my relief we heard the other girl coming towards us. Knowing there would be time for me to say nothing more, to answer no more questions, I said:

'Yes.'

CHAPTER VIII

FROZEN LEAVES

I went out into the night again, and was not surprised, being full of brandy, to find that I did not feel cold. The wind was still blowing and the sky was black. Returning, I walked on the side of the road near the river. I passed the railings of a small public garden and saw that someone had left the gate open. I felt isolated in the night: the time had passed for going to bed and I might just as well be anywhere. I walked into the garden, along a gravel path between narrow allotments: there was a smell of old cabbage stalks and dead bonfires. I could see a statue, big and heavy like those in Parliament Square. I made for the Embankment wall, and looked down at the water. I thought of Julia, and was haunted by an echo – a lost soul. A gust of wind blew some leaves round my feet again.

I stayed still. I was filled with recollections from my past. My memory stirred with pictures of the world in which Julia lived, where men and women swept from place to place in insistent promiscuity. I knew something about it. I had once spent a season there myself. I had quitted it long since, and looking back on it I usually found it strange and remote – yet sometimes, as at this moment, it felt very near, as if a life off the rails were only a single jump, a single chance, from a life on them.

It was after I had been finally rejected by My Last One that I had decided in anguish to take anyone who wanted me. Not the action of a sane man? I quite agree. If it comes to that, are you sane all of the time? In a wild fit I wanted to humiliate myself, to destroy my romantic hopes and my self-respect. The results were remarkable.

When I entered the world of insistent promiscuity I first of all got some surprises. And then I found myself observing things about human nature that I had never known before. I came, I saw, I learned. What I learned would have roused in some people hatred and disgust. I came to feel neither. I was invaded by a poignant sympathy instead.

I saw men and women searching desperately for something they never found. I did not know what it was they were looking for, nor often did they. The place where they searched was in others: they never found it. I listened to their fantastic stories – having got their main preoccupation off their chests, they were always ready for a good long talk to me. I saw that they never found what they were looking for in others – it was not there. I began to realise it could not be. What they were really looking for was something in themselves, and – here was the tragedy – it was not there either.

Like a swirl of leaves they rattled along from bed to bed, sofa to floor, taxi to telephone-box – in pursuit of the act of love. I have to say that whatever else they missed, they found plenty of copulation. But the act of love is what it was not. It was not an act of passion or sensation as often as all that. It was more like an act of domination and curiosity – and because for all but the coldest of us that is not enough, it was nearly always shot through with unformulated hope. Hope that this performance might miraculously turn into an act of love.

And so they went on. Something was missing, something was incapable, within themselves. Just a few of them seemed to me to have no hearts at all; many, many had hearts that were strained and frozen.

My recollections seemed to surround me like an atmosphere, while I leaned against the massive stone wall and gazed across the river. I imagined Julia, high up in her lighted room, trying to compose her anxious conflicting mind for sleep. A lost soul – she did not notice that the single jump between the life she led and the life she hoped for was across a chasm. In her imagination she saw herself being faithful to a loving husband, while all the time she was hurrying down the raffish by-ways of sex. The romantic hope and the reality had fallen completely apart.

The tide was high, flapping harshly against the stone just

beneath me: occasionally the wind brought up a stale earthy whiff from the water. I found myself thinking about Robert, then about myself, myself and Myrtle. The wind went on blowing, cutting between the brim of my hat and the edge of my collar. With the street lamps well behind me I could see a few stars in the sky. Lighted windows, stars, lost souls, broken hearts – somehow, in spite of everything, I was feeling uplifted. I looked round. Somebody else was leaning against the wall at the other end of the garden.

I was startled. I thought it must be a man because there was no gleam of light stockings. He was quite motionless. He must have been there all the while, brooding in the middle of the night. I wondered what on earth he could be brooding about – must be crazy, I thought. His figure turned from the wall and walked quietly away. And I, who a moment before had been imagining I knew some of the secrets of others, was confronted by the utter separateness of us all, the incredible mysteriousness of one to another.

I stayed on, still feeling warm inside my overcoat and uplifted in heart. I remember thinking what a good name *eau de vie* was. The lights across the river swayed in the wind, a lorry thundered along the Embankment, once I heard voices. I stayed because the afflatus was growing stronger. Everything that had happened to me seemed close at hand. Suffering, humiliation, heartbreak – I contemplated them with powerful emotion. I had survived them all. Instead of having died I was living. What is more, I felt certain I was growing. It seemed that even the most dreadful experiences of life could make one bigger, could make one know more and finally embrace more.

The effects of the brandy must have been powerfully resurgent. I remember most vividly that I looked up at the sky and the stars.

'The universe is expanding,' I thought, 'and so am I.'

CHAPTER IX

THE PLACE ON A LIST

Next morning Robert left London for a fortnight. He took Julia with him. I did not know what was going on, as he went away without my seeing him first.

'There isn't a great deal to do in the office,' he said on the telephone. 'Come down to Brighton if you want to see me.'

Robert always told me there was not very much to do in the office whenever he went away. It would have distressed him to think that he was over-burdening me with his work.

Robert's voice became solemn. 'I'm going to begin planning a novel.'

I exclaimed in surprise, having had fornication firmly fixed in my mind.

Robert's solemnity increased. 'It's time one of us made a start.'

I stopped laughing. For one thing his remark made our break with regular employment seem closer, for another it piqued me because I had already begun a plan of my own in secret.

'Good luck to you, old boy,' I said, and it came from my heart.

'We'll get there in the end,' said Robert.

And so I began the day's work. Our personal assistant came in, a plump young woman with an admirable desire to please and not quite enough organising power. She said Mr Froggatt wanted to see me.

Mr Froggatt was our Senior Executive Officer. People in the class of Robert and me were employed to make decisions on policy: people in Froggatt's class were employed to carry them out. Thus it will be seen that Robert and I belonged to the classiest class of the service, Froggatt to the one below it. But Froggatt was near the highest grade of his class and therefore something of a power in his way. In my own mind I thought of him as our chief henchman. I liked him because he was equable and well-disposed.

I ensconced myself at my desk to receive him, and opened the heaviest file in sight. I was not above trying to make an impression on the lower orders, just like any member of the classiest class inside the government service or outside it, although I was aware that Froggatt knew perfectly well what files must be on my bench since he had sent them to me. I assumed a grave expression.

Froggatt came in. He too assumed a grave expression – he always did when he came to see me. It seemed to me ridiculous that before exchanging a word we should both look grave, but there it was.

Froggatt spoke in a slow, melodious, submissive voice. 'I'm glad you were able to see me, Mr ——' He addressed me by my surname, which is Lunn.

'That's all right, Froggatt. What's the matter?' I saw that he was holding a sheet of paper.

'It's about Dr Chubb, sir.' Froggatt glanced over his shoulder at the second desk which had been placed at the far end of my room, against the window which looked into the well of the building.

'Oh.'

'He came back last night, and was very upset by this, I believe.' Froggatt came towards me holding out the document. 'I thought I would like to see you before Dr Chubb came in.' He handed the document over. 'You'll no doubt have seen it already.'

I glanced at it. 'No.' It was a staff-chart.

Froggatt continued in his slow melodious submissive way. 'Well, we do circulate you with all such information, sir.' He was rebuking me, if not actually applying correction.

'Well, I don't read it all,' I said. 'So you can circulate it till you're blue in the face.'

Froggatt gave me an imperturbable stately smile. 'Ah, Mr Lunn, I hardly think I am likely to change colour in such a way.'

It was one of Froggatt's characteristic habits to treat my racy exaggerations literally. I restrained myself from uttering an improper word. What held me back was not my having been taught never to use such words before subordinates: it was a conviction that Froggatt would be secretly delighted to hear me do it.

'What am I supposed to discover from this?'

'I believe Dr Chubb is somewhat dissatisfied with the position of his name.' Froggatt took a breath, and went on at an even slower pace. 'Before Dr Chubb comes in, I should like to say – '

Froggatt never said what he would like to say, because at that moment Chubb came in. He greeted me while taking off his fine black hat and his beautiful navy-blue overcoat – though Chubb could never look either handsome or specially gentlemanly, his clothes were perfect. Froggatt made a genteel exit.

Chubb promptly made an exit as well. He took his towel and his little soap-box. He had a preoccupation with hygiene. I was left to survey the chart, which set forth the hierarchy of our division.

For anyone who does not know, I ought to explain that such charts are always being circulated in the government service. They look like genealogical trees, and fulfil the apparently insatiable desire of all human beings to know where they stand – not, I may say, that such knowledge brings either peace or satisfaction. With the object of seeing that you stand a cut above some of your fellows, you find you stand a cut below others.

Dr Chubb, reporting to Robert as I did, had been shown on the same level as me. Whereas he was senior to me. His name was printed a quarter of an inch lower down the sheet than it should have been.

'Oh dear!' I said aloud. Accidents of this kind seemed to happen most frequently to people whose dignity was most susceptible to affront. To me the quarter of an inch would have made little difference one way or the other. Had the whole division been shown reporting to Froggatt I would not have minded – in fact it would not have been a bad idea, since Froggatt was nothing if not sensible. To Dr Chubb, a humble ambitious man, whose life had been devoted to small advancements, whose career was an accumulation of quarter inches, I knew the mistake was grave.

Chubb came in again, put away his towel and little soap-box, and came towards me. His expression spoke for him. His rosy cheeks, instead of being fixed in his habitual nervous smile, were drawn in. His teeth were not visible, and over the half-moons of his spectacles his eyes were popping with alarm.

'I'm sorry about this,' I said.

'I don't want you to think that I wish to make heavy weather over this kind of thing, because, as you'll understand,' said Chubb, 'I'm not the sort of person who does make heavy weather over, over this kind of thing ... but I should like to say, before we go any further – you'll appreciate the position I'm in – '

'Yes,' I said, while he took a breath.

Chubb finished a very long sentence, whose syntax I cannot vouch for.

'I'll tell Froggatt to get it corrected,' I said.

Chubb was not in the least satisfied. 'I really felt this was the kind of thing which ought to be brought to the notice of Sir Francis and actually I've written him a letter to that effect. I tried to see him personally.' Chubb stared at me with his gravest and most detached expression of alarm. 'It was impossible.' He paused. 'Now, I don't want to criticise the department – I feel rather uncertain of my position here, as you may guess, for various reasons – but I do feel that it should be possible to arrange to see the head on urgent personal matters without having to wait two and a half weeks for an appointment. It was only through a fortunate coincidence that I happened to run into him, coming out of the lavatory, and was able to mention briefly what had occurred.' He paused, and his tone took a note almost of horror. 'I'm afraid he put me off.'

I suddenly had an inspiration. 'You should try getting at him through James Irskine.' It seemed to me that by all the rules Chubb and James were bound to get at loggerheads –

who was I to keep nature from taking its proper course?

'Do you think so?' said Chubb.

I nodded. At that moment there was a rap on the door. We both turned to see James come in.

'Sorry to interrupt. I've had a word with Sir Francis' – he glanced at me with a faint gleam in his glaring blue eyes – 'while he was taking off his hat and coat.' He turned to Chubb. 'About you.'

'Ah,' said Chubb, hopefully.

'About this list. It was before Lunn came in. I got on to Froggatt, and told him D.O.R.R.S. wanted the old list withdrawn and a new one circulated. Correct, this time.'

It was clear that James thought Dr Chubb would be satisfied. Not a bit of it. Chubb immediately embarked on a long speech about his apprehensions. I cannot say he touched on his points. As I listened I compared him with Froggatt. If both were given a point to make, which would take the longer, Chubb with his remarkable prolixity or Froggatt with his immoderately slow articulation?

'...I'm sure I don't want to make difficulties, but you'll understand that I feel bound in certain circumstances – although I naturally don't feel certain of myself in this organisation – to put forward my point of view...'

I had no idea what Chubb was getting at. I had time to watch James, to admire the masculine stance of a man who is satisfied with his own intelligence, looks, virility and prospective success in affairs. I perceived that his angry glare did undergo just detectable variations as Chubb's jeremiad proceeded. His face went redder. There was not the slightest doubt that in due course Chubb and James would come into a furious head-on collision over some matter of correct Civil Service procedure. The quarrel would not affect either of their careers: it would just make a powerful addition to their daily lives.

Chubb really was leading up to something. His voice was filling out and he was getting a hunted look in the eyes.

'I agree that you have a case,' James said, with wooden impatience. 'It will be put right.'

'That's not the point,' said Chubb. 'That isn't what I'm

trying to express. What I'm trying to express is this.' Suddenly, in the outburst of naked emotion his prolixity fell away. 'This would never have happened,' he cried, *'if I'd had a room of my own!'*

CHAPTER X

AN OFFICE CHAIR

'Tell Mr Froggatt I want to see him,' I said to my personal assistant, as soon as James had stalked out of the room.

Froggatt came in, looking diffident. He was a man aged about forty, narrow across the shoulders and narrow all the way down. He had a long face with big eyes a bit like a bloodhound's, and he carried his head forward a little.

'Did you want me, sir?'

As Froggatt stood in front of me, I glanced at Chubb, who was sitting at his desk, apparently composing a memorandum with his own hand. I picked up the offending chart.

I said: 'If I do read this kind of document, I expect it to be correct.'

'Yes, Mr Lunn, I quite understand your irritation. First of all I should like to explain how – '

'Please don't!' I said. 'Whenever anything goes wrong in the government service, dozens of people spend valuable time on a protracted post-mortem. It doesn't stop them making the same mistake again. No, Froggatt' – he was about to try and put a word in – 'I don't want to hear explanations, analyses or reasons. I want to hear that it won't happen again.'

'I agree that excuses – '

'It's the future I'm interested in, not the past.'

A slight pause. 'Quite.' Froggatt had given up. Instead of looking stately and slyly submissive he was injured and abashed. 'I'll do my best. I'm afraid I haven't time for everything.'

'There's something else I want you to do, Froggatt.' I had another kind of trick to play on him. 'Dr Chubb is going to be in London. Will you make arrangements for him to have an office of his own?'

Immediately Froggatt's expression changed. I must explain that Froggatt had a weakness for making our staff frequently change offices. They disliked it. Most men and women get used to their place in an office, to their bench, their chair, the position of the window, the people sitting on either side of them. It was quite a while before I tumbled to what Froggatt was doing by moving them. I did not dream of interfering, even when his manoeuvres broke up the division's most romantic, if illicit, love-affair. He was showing the staff he was their master. Froggatt's expression change to alert interest. 'Yes?' he said in a soft low tone, which I noted with pleasure.

We were interrupted. Chubb rose from his desk and came towards us.

'I hope you don't mind my butting in like this,' he said, smiling toothily. 'I don't want to make everyone a great deal of trouble over this question of rooms. After all, I shall be out of London much of the time during the next few weeks in the continuance of my present duties.'

'I don't think it will cause us much trouble,' said Froggatt, looking at me for approval and support.

'I've been giving some thought to this matter,' said Chubb, 'and it occurred to me that in view of Your Friend' – Chubb always referred thus to Robert – 'being away from his office for considerable periods – in view of his only being here part-time – it might be thought more suitable for me to occupy his office during his absence. On the advent of his return I could move back here.'

Froggatt and I glanced at each other. I did not know him well enough to be certain that he was thinking exactly the same as me: it was probably along the same lines. Everyone in the higher ranks of the government service knows that he allows someone else to occupy his office chair at his peril. If the secret history of the Second World War had an appendix showing the names of distinguished persons who left their offices on interesting expeditions and returned to find someone else in their chairs for good, no boss would ever budge from Whitehall again.

'I should like you to have an office really of your own,' I said weightily. 'We can't risk any more mistakes like this.'

Chubb hesitated nervously. At that moment he had just insufficient push.

'I think I can do as Mr Lunn wishes, without much difficulty,' said Froggatt. He knew just the right moment for that kind of move.

'Well,' said Chubb, 'I put it forward as a suggestion.'

'Thank you,' I said, warmly. 'It's very considerate of you.'

I knew that that was the end of it.

Froggatt went out. Chubb returned to his desk, and started to write again.

At first I was occupied with trying to decide whether Chubb, even when he was writing, looked through the lenses of his spectacles. And then I fell into thoughts of a deeper and more entertaining kind. 'So he'd like to plant his not inconsiderable seat in Robert's chair,' I thought. 'Now that's interesting!'

CHAPTER XI

AN UNUSUAL OFFER

The weeks were passing and the time was getting nearer for Haxby's demobilisation. I became steadily more agitated. I had persuaded Myrtle to promise she would ask him for a divorce the moment she saw him.

There was no doubt that Myrtle did not want to ask her husband for a divorce – she wanted to so little that she made great efforts not to think about it. My agitation was not diminished by such tactics. I simply could not see how, with the best will in the world, she could marry me without previously being divorced from Haxby. To me her divorce was the *clou* of our whole situation: I could not help explaining this to her.

Myrtle gave me a look of reproach and then fell into distant melancholy silence.

I thought if only Myrtle had been trained in the Civil Service she would have understood how necessary action was before results could ensue.

Myrtle had a tender nature. She was very distressed at the thought of hurting Haxby. Her reluctance once showed signs of breaking down, while she was considering whether it was sometimes necessary to be cruel to be kind.

Unfortunately I observed that you never had to be cruel to be kind, though you often had to be cruel to get what you wanted – poor Myrtle was horrified.

There followed distant melancholy silence for at least half an hour, during which her tender sensitive nature wrapped itself up again in a warm veil of obstinacy.

I tried hard to understand Myrtle's nature during this period. The more I tried, the less able I found myself to follow it. I was humble. Robert had already established by disputation that I was the crazy unrealistic partner and Myrtle the shrewd down-to-earth one. I really ought to have been able to understand Myrtle.

In the first place I discovered that Myrtle was taking quite seriously the possibility of Haxby's not surviving the fighting in Palestine. I was sure she would mourn his sacrifice for the rest of her life, permitting herself the consolation of marrying me after a discreet interval of widowhood. The idea flitted constantly through her mind, like a perfect solution. However, widowhood, like perfection, turned out to be unattainable. When there was no sign of intervention by either Jews or Arabs, Myrtle began to have hopes of the War Office: she thought Haxby's date of demobilisation might be put back. I could see no justification for such an idea. I had been demobilised myself: you were given a number, and when in due rotation your number came up, you were out. Myrtle found in this concept merely another sign of my mechanical mind.

The weeks passed, and the Cabinet made no sudden declaration that from tomorrow all demobilisation would cease. Myrtle began to wonder if Haxby would decide to stay in the Army of his own accord. She had strong arguments in favour: Haxby had no job to come home to, and, as Myrtle said, he was good at being a soldier – he had risen from Private to Captain in the R.A.S.C. On the other hand it was clear to me that Haxby had hated Army life from the moment he was called up, had never ceased to grumble about it, and was now entirely given up to waiting for his demobilisation day.

Do you begin to see why I found it hard to understand Myrtle, and impossible to follow her? Was this a difference, I asked myself, between a crazy unrealistic person and a shrewd down-to-earth one who could believe in miracles? It was most puzzling. For, take my word for it, Myrtle reached the stage of hoping for events that could arise only from divine intervention. It was like living with someone just about to go bankrupt who was constantly awaiting an unexpected legacy of one hundred thousand pounds, free of duty.

I was sorry for Myrtle, and the further she retired into her dreams of reprieve the less I said about it. I ceased to mention either Haxby or divorce. Myrtle seemed happier.

Towards the middle of December, Myrtle and I went to the wedding of one of her professional colleagues. It was a smart wedding of milliners in Caxton Hall. The bride was wearing a hat that looked like a miniature sitting pheasant. The other women's hats were so fashionable that they did not look like hats at all, but more like objects which bore no known relation to the human head, such as pagodas and wheel-barrows. For all her sophistication, Myrtle was enchanted to be there. Her eyes glowed with a romantic light. She squeezed my arm. She introduced me to some of her acquaintances. 'This is my young man.' I could only assume that they did not know she had a husband or that she had forgotten.

Myrtle and I happened to come out a little in advance of the bride and bridegroom. One of the disconcerting features of a registry office wedding is the absence of a clearly defined beginning and end to the ceremony. In a church wedding the organ tootles so loudly that even the drunks know when they have to go in and come out. Myrtle and I found ourselves in the porch of the building while the bride and bridegroom were still doing something inside. Some of the other guests were moving along behind us, and we saw two press photographers going past in the opposite direction. At the top of the steps we paused and looked round.

It was a cold dark morning, with occasional bursts of sunshine lighting up the bombed-out church on the opposite side of the road. There was something cheerless and inhuman about the white mosaic steps and heavy metal canopy of the porch – they reminded me of the entrance to a technical college. Myrtle was delighted all the same.

Suddenly a taxi drew up and a scruffy young man in a duffel-coat jumped out, carrying a camera and flash-bulb. He spotted Myrtle and me in the centre of the group, Myrtle with her hair elegantly adorned by a length of dark green net and me with a red carnation in my buttonhole.

'Excuse me, are you the newly-weds?'

Myrtle said: 'Yes.'

And our photographs were taken.

I denied it immediately. The photographer was cross. Some of the other guests laughed. Myrtle laughed with satisfaction. At that moment the true bride and bridegroom came out and posed.

Instead of waiting for one of the cars to the reception, Myrtle and I took a taxi in Victoria Street. In the taxi I remonstrated with her.

All that Myrtle said was: 'Darling, I wished it really was us.'

I could not help feeling a little mollified, and yet I could not help feeling a little frightened. I looked at Myrtle's profile, at her soft easy smile as she snuggled against my shoulder. I did not doubt she was imagining that we were driving away from our own wedding, our own – if I may say so – bigamous wedding. In a way she was right. How much easier it would have been to forget she had a husband whom she must divorce before she could marry me, how much less painful! I sympathised with her. She was not alone either. I pictured all the host of bigamists I read about every Sunday in *The News of the World*. Now I came to think about it, I was puzzled. Myrtle and I could have come out of the Caxton Hall and faced the world with ease at last. Mr and Mrs Lunn. All we were asking was the opportunity to make an honest man and woman of ourselves. What *was* wrong with bigamy?

The taxi emerged from Buckingham Palace Road and we saw a fleeting glow of sunlight on the façade of the Palace. I kissed Myrtle. Myrtle kissed me. What were we to do? What was our solution? Divorce, with its mixture of pain and moral obloquy?

We were silent. The taxi drove on towards St James's – we were making for the Mayfair Hotel. The smile faded from Myrtle's face, and I could tell she was thinking seriously. I stroked her hand, and whispered, 'Darling'.

Beside the Ritz we were held up by traffic lights. It was dark inside the taxi because the street was narrow. Myrtle leaned away from me a little. I glanced at her and saw that she was looking at me.

'What is it?'

Myrtle spoke with difficulty. 'Darling, would you like me to
 . . . . just come and live with you.' She stopped, and her eyelids

fluttered down.

'You mean, set up together without being married?'

Myrtle looked away. It was what she did mean.

Only some time later did I see how time had turned the tables on me. It was the offer that once I had made to Myrtle. Now, as I heard her making the offer to me, I could hardly keep back the emotion I felt.

'Darling!' I cried. 'That wouldn't do at all!'

Myrtle glanced at me. In the half-light I could not see whether she was giving me a look of surprise or reproach or sympathy. The taxi suddenly jerked forward to cross Piccadilly.

'I want you to marry me,' I said. 'Darling, the answer's No.'

CHAPTER XII

THROUGH A CARRIAGE-WINDOW

Haxby landed in England on Christmas Eve. Myrtle spent the day in London with me. My office closed down at mid-day, and Myrtle and I walked round, looking in the lighted shop-windows. She had a telegram saying which train from Euston Haxby hoped to catch, and she intended to join him on it.

'We don't know if he'll get there in time,' she said. I felt dreadfully tense. We did not mention the fact that she had got to tell him at last. While we were sitting in a café, waiting for the waitress to bring our tea, she looked at me with a tremulous light in her eyes, and said:

'I wish it were you instead of me.'

I squeezed her fingers. There was nothing to say.

After tea Myrtle bought herself some suede boots lined with sheepskin. It seemed to comfort her. The boots were expensive. She shook her head sadly – she was convinced that we were going to have a desperately cold winter.

I bought a diary. I did not need it. I bought it because it somehow brought nearer the date when all our troubles would be over. Tonight Haxby would know. In January the divorce proceedings would start. We should have to wait through February, March, April – it was taking four or five months to get a divorce, sometimes longer. But the summer! Opening the diary at July seemed to let out the sunny glow of a millenium.

I took Myrtle to the station. It was about half-past seven, snowy, dark and slightly foggy. Crowds of people were arriving at Euston. There were taxis and lights and bright faces. The first thing we saw just inside the colonnade was a great pile of Christmas trees, lying horizontally with their sombre green branches entwined and circles of brown timber shining where the stems had been cut off. There were parcels on trucks, in children's hands, everywhere. There was the familiar fishy smell, and an occasional whiff of oranges. I took Myrtle to her train. It was very early.

Myrtle chose a seat in a comfortable new coach: the compartments had wide windows on the platform side. Myrtle got out again and walked with me to the end of the platform, so that I could kiss her in the darkness. I was hasty. I did not want Haxby to see us, and somehow I wanted to part from her as quickly as possible so that the scene could begin.

At last Myrtle let me go. From the platform I watched her sit down beside the window. I waved and walked away.

I saw Haxby. He was standing at a bookstall, choosing a book. He was in uniform. I strode past.

Off the platform, I went to one of the refreshment rooms and bought myself a drink. I had an evening newspaper but I could not bring myself to read it. I kept looking at the clock.

A quarter of an hour went by. The train was nearly due to leave. I felt an impulse that I could not resist. I went out, bought another platform ticket, turned up the collar of my overcoat, and once more went down the length of the train. The lights inside were bright. Through the windows you could see all the people. I kept in the shadows. I felt furtive. I came to the compartment where Myrtle and Haxby were. I saw them.

They were chatting together amicably.

PART III

CHAPTER I

A QUESTION OF EMPLOYMENT

It was three weeks before I saw Myrtle again. I had spent them in Switzerland, and I prayed that Myrtle had spent them in reconciling Haxby to his fate.

We met by secret pre-arrangement at the Carlos. I went straight there from the air-terminal. It was about eight o'clock in the evening. The streets of London were patchy with snow and looked to me discouragingly dark after Zürich and Geneva. As I got out of the taxi a few damp flakes fell on my head.

The porch of the hotel was glowing. A commissionaire came out to look after my luggage, and asked me if I was going to stay. I said not.

The first person I set eyes on was Myrtle. There was a chair placed in full view of the entrance: it was high-backed and sweeping-armed, suitable for Hamlet to soliloquise in. Myrtle was sitting in it, holding a glass.

'Darling!' she cried. There was a big vase full of white and yellow chrysanthemums behind her head. Her eyes were shining and her lips were parted. We embraced.

I stood back and looked at her. She was wearing a new dress. She was looking excited and happy. She was a trifle tipsy.

'Your aeroplane was terribly late,' she said. 'They've been telephoning the airport every quarter of an hour for me.' She smiled. 'There was nothing else to do but drink.' At that she dropped her eyelids. She lifted them just in time to see my luggage being carried in. 'Darling! You're going to stay here? I am. I've got a room.'

I took off my overcoat and handed it in. Myrtle watched me.

Certainly she was a trifle tipsy. There was not the slightest trace of the over-awed look she usually wore in the Carlos. Her new dress was beautiful. I slipped my arm round her waist and led her towards an alcove in one of the lounges.

'What do you think of my hair?' she asked. 'Rudolf's latest style.' She noticed a waiter passing, and skilfully gave him her glass. 'Tell George we want two more of the same.' She turned to me. 'It's something special he mixed me. I told him I was waiting for you.'

We sat down side by side on a sofa which filled the alcove.

'Darling,' I said, because she looked so happy: 'Everything's all right?'

'Everything?' She looked at me suddenly, her eyes big and round and golden.

'You've told Dennis?' I said. 'He agrees?'

There was silence, between Myrtle and me complete silence.

The waiter came up and placed two glasses on a low table before us. I paid him and he went away. The drinks were amber-coloured – they stood untouched.

'You haven't told him yet?' I said.

'You can see I haven't.'

'Darling, why?'

Myrtle put her hand to her forehead as if she had a headache. My prayers had been in vain, as not only was Haxby not reconciled to his fate – he did not even know yet what it was. For a moment I began to wonder what it was myself. It hung on Myrtle. If it came to that, my own fate hung on Myrtle. There was a long pause.

'Aren't you going to try my drink?' Myrtle spoke as if the incident were closed. Alcohol had given her unaccustomed resilience. She picked up her glass to acquire more of it.

I tried the drink, and put it down again. The incident was not closed. I said:

'Aren't you going to tell me why you haven't told him?'

'Darling, I couldn't!'

'But you'll have to.'

'It's too soon. He's only just got back. He's so at a loss...'

Much as I loved Myrtle I could not help wishing her conversation had a little more edge.

I said: 'Do you mean he's at a loss trying to fit into civilian life?', thinking what a stupid remark it was.

'Yes, that's just it,' said Myrtle.

'I had to fit into it.'

'You're different.'

'I don't see why.'

'You had a job to come to, but he hasn't.'

I was dismayed. 'He'll get one,' I said comfortably, but without conviction.

'Of course he will.' Myrtle turned on me. 'You were lucky.'

'Indeed!' I said crossly.

Myrtle sipped her drink again. I swallowed the whole of mine in two gulps.

'Darling,' Myrtle said, changing her tone, 'I can't leave him until he's got a job. I couldn't bear to do it.'

'Do you really mean that?' I said at last.

'Yes.' A gentle, tremulous, entirely obstinate yes.

I now had something else to think about. My fate hung on Myrtle – it hung also on Haxby's getting a job. I for one had no idea what he could be employed as. It was comic: it was appalling.

'What sort of a job is he looking for?'

'He doesn't really know.' Myrtle paused. 'Do you think you could order another drink, darling?' She paused again. 'I want to ask your advice.'

I told you Myrtle was capable of earning a lot of money in business. Now do you see why? I did not know whether to burst into laughter or to box her ears. I did neither. Myrtle had signalled the waiter, so I ordered some more drinks. I leaned my head on the cushion of the sofa. On a ledge that ran round the alcove there was a bunch of paper-white narcissus, I just caught their clear frail scent. I thought of spring, the time for all such exquisite flowers, the time for Myrtle's divorce.

'Hadn't you better tell them you want a room for the night?' Myrtle said gently, 'You can't sleep in mine' – she gave a lubricious sigh. 'It's only a single bed.'

The drinks arrived. I sat up.

'What sort of a job?' I repeated.

'He'd like to be a journalist,' said Myrtle. She went on. 'He's edited his unit's newspaper terribly well. The CO congratulated him.'

I recalled that when she married him he was a reporter on the local newspaper. I said nothing.

'And he knows an awful lot about music,' she said. 'Especially on records. I think he could do terribly well on the BBC – you know, putting on a programme of gramophone records.'

'A disc-jockey!' I cried.

'How could he become one?' said Myrtle.

I will not record the rest of the conversation. Any man's blood might run cold at the prospect of his marriage depending on his future wife's present husband getting a job as a putter-on of gramophone records.

But Myrtle's intention was perfectly real, to me deplorably real. Her tender nature revolted from deserting her husband when he had no means of supporting himself. Quite rightly. Yet there was something else. I had led her to believe in the past, when she tried to make me jealous, that I did not think much of him, and she hated it. Even though she was going to divorce him. Her vanity was wounded. Now I had got to take him seriously. 'But as a potential disc-jockey!' I thought: 'That's the limit!'

I said gravely: 'I think we must ask Robert to help.'

'Do you!' Myrtle's face lighted instantly, naively. She put her hand on mine. 'He really will get a job,' she said, 'and then I shan't mind telling him half so much.'

I said nothing. What she read in my face satisfied her.

'I think you need some dinner, darling,' she said. There was a lurking smile round the corners of her mouth. 'I must say I do.'

We made our way to the dining-room, with its softly-lit mahogany walls, but my thoughts were elsewhere. I was recalling the number of scenes in which I had begged Myrtle to tell her husband we wanted to be married. The scenes caused her distress. What is more, they caused her patent satisfaction. I asked myself an unpleasant question. 'How many more of them are there to be?'

CHAPTER II

IN THE STALLS-BAR

Robert invited me to go to the theatre with him and Julia. We were to see a performance of *Love For Love* at the Haymarket theatre, and Julia was to meet us in the stalls-bar – it was Robert's way of side-stepping her efforts to make him put on evening dress and take her to dine at the Savoy afterwards. I was sworn to tell Julia, when a suitable moment arose, that I had brought Robert straight from the office. We had been quietly enjoying sandwiches and beer in a public-house round the corner.

I recalled earlier days when Robert had been delighted to put on his evening dress and flaunt Julia in fashionable places. I attached no unusual importance to this change, since I had seen it happen with all his other young women. He loved to be seen with them in public – remember he only chose pretty ones. But they never knew when he had had enough of it, chiefly, I am afraid, because they had never had enough themselves.

The Haymarket is one of London's most beautiful theatres: we thought it was perfect. As we went up the steps we felt the romantic thrill of having history around us – in imagination we were going to see a play written by Robert or me. One's own play performed at the Haymarket – perfection indeed!

We went down the corridor towards the bar and Robert glanced at his watch. It was not quite early enough for him to have gone home to change, not quite late enough to prevent his having a drink before the show. He nodded his big head with satisfaction.

It was a spacious bar, carpeted and lit by chandeliers. The two halves of the room were on different levels with a couple of steps between. Standing on the steps gave us a slight feeling of grandeur, so we stood there.

The choice of play was Julia's, not Robert's nor mine.

'It doesn't follow,' he said loftily, 'that girls whose tastes are far from highbrow in certain other matters, don't have remarkably highbrow tastes in literature.' And then he reminded me of one of my young women whom I would hear reciting passages from Shakespeare as I dropped off to sleep. Long passages.

There was a stir beside us. Julia had arrived.

Her eyes were brightly transparent and the skin of her neck was flushed. 'Robert, darling, get me a drink!'

While she was waiting she glanced at me furtively. 'It's the first one I've had today.'

I offered her a cigarette. She took it. There were some particles of face-powder on the front of her dress. It was the red silk dress I had seen before.

'I've just heard from Wladislaw!'

At that moment Robert returned. Julia took the glass and drank. She said:

'Wladislaw's just rung me up.'

'Where is he?'

'In Paris.'

Suddenly there was a silence.

Robert said impatiently: 'What does he want?'

'To prevent me from marrying you.' Julia shook her head, as if she were angry. Her hair swung against her cheeks.

Robert's expression changed completely. 'Have you told him?'

'Yes.'

Robert was silent. Julia stared at him with her head down, but his face showed no emotion. I glanced round the bar: it was getting quite full.

'You knew I was going to,' Julia said.

'I knew you wanted to,' said Robert.

'You knew that for me that's the same thing,' said Julia. 'You told me so, yourself.'

I was delighted to see Robert hoist with his own petard. He pretended to be thinking about something else.

Julia's tone changed.

'We've got to get things straight, darling.'

Robert still did not reply. He was no believer in the implicit virtue of straightness in private affairs.

'I didn't tell him who you were,' Julia said. 'I told him I'd got my first chance of real happiness.'

'He'll find out quickly enough when he gets back.'

'What does that matter? He's got to know, sometime.' She burst out passionately. 'He's got to let me have my chance!'

I said: 'Surely he can't prevent you?'

Julia looked startled.

Robert said: 'What is he proposing to do?'

Julia said: 'He thinks he's going to prove to you that I'm married to him.'

Robert and I caught each other's eye.

I said: 'But he can't. To prove you're married to him, he'd have to produce the marriage lines.'

'There are none!' said Julia, triumphantly.

'Good.'

'I can produce the documents about my change of name.'

'Better.'

'I won't sit down under it!'

Julia finished her drink. Robert took the glass and went down to the bar-counter.

'I've sat down under it long enough.'

'Under what?'

'Wladislaw's attempts to prevent me getting out of his clutches.'

'I don't see how he can hold you.'

Julia did not reply. She was looking away. Wladislaw had got some kind of hold on her, on her imagination, on her body – I was sure he was a man of powerful direct personality.

Julia turned to me. 'I don't think Robert's as strong as he ought to be.'

'Oh.'

'He doesn't help me.'

'I don't see what he can do.' This was not true. I thought a definite proposal of marriage would have helped.

'I do!' said Julia, with force.

I glanced down at Robert, who was having to wait at the

bar.

'Then you mustn't demand it,' I said. 'Robert *has* got a strong personality.' Julia looked at me with attention. 'But it's indirect,' I went on: 'He's subtle and tricky and evasive, but he's obstinate and determined. He'll do what *he* wants.'

Julia blinked: her expression hardened. My explanation, like most of my explanations of people to each other, appeared to convey next to no meaning while having a markedly irritant effect.

I said quietly: 'He's enquiring about buying houses.' That sort of explanation could never go wrong.

Julia's face softened as quickly as it had hardened. 'In Mayfair?'

'Yes.'

Robert rejoined us. He said, thoughtfully: 'Did you find out what were the results of Wladislaw's researches in Poland?'

'Yes. He says he now has proof that his wife was killed.'

'H'm.'

Julia said: 'He's always got proof of something.'

Robert's eye suddenly sparkled. 'I suspect he's a man for me to deal with.' He was already thinking of the wily circuits he would make round Czyz.

Julia smiled at him admiringly.

'It would have been easier,' said Robert, 'if he'd found proof that she was alive.'

'He's terribly honest,' said Julia. She paused. 'He's got no sense of humour and he's terribly honest. It's an awful combination.'

'That doesn't matter.' Robert dismissed her momentarily. His imagination was moving. I glanced at Julia, because it occurred to me that she had little idea of which way it was moving. Czyz was not the only person round whom wily circuits would be made.

'It does if you have to live with him,' Julia said.

Robert suddenly glanced at her with a kind of amused concentration. 'It didn't suit you too badly.'

'I don't know what you mean!' Julia took offence.

'A man with that kind of temperament doesn't need much encouragement to burst into passionate quarrelling.'

'So you think that's what I want?'

'It's what you got. On the whole people get what they want in that way.'

'I've never had a quarrel with you!' Julia's voice broke out. Some people who were standing nearby turned and looked at us. The men continued to look at Julia.

Robert said in a low voice: 'That's because I have a strong sense of humour and am not specially honest.'

'I shall make you quarrel when we're married!'

I thought she would not find it easy. When he was really angry Robert fell into penetratingly gloomy, white-faced silence.

The first warning-bell for the play rang inside the bar. Julia began to sip the remainder of her drink.

Robert said: 'When is Wladislaw due back in London?'

'I couldn't hear him. That was what I wanted to catch most, but the line suddenly got worse. But don't worry – he'll ring again before he leaves Paris. He'll ring every night.'

I saw a suspicious look cross Robert's face.

'Anyway, it doesn't matter,' Julia said: 'He won't be coming back to the flat.'

Immediately I pricked up my ears. It ought to have occurred to me long ago that Wladislaw paid the rent of Julia's flat.

'He'll probably demand to,' said Robert.

'I shall tell him I want my girl-friend to stay. She hasn't got anywhere else to go.'

'She could find somewhere.'

'She isn't going to.'

'If he asks her to leave, she'll have to.'

'You don't see my point of view!'

'I do, my dear.'

'Robert, if you did, you wouldn't be able to even contemplate Wladislaw's coming to live in the flat again.' She looked away. 'If he does, I won't sit down under it! I'll sleep behind bolted doors!'

Robert grinned.

For an instant Julia was poised on the brink of fury. Her grip tightened on her glass. Then suddenly she burst into laughter.

'It would be the first time since I was fifteen.' Her face warmed most attractively with a careless, detached amusement.

The second warning-bell rang. I noticed that most of the other people had left the bar. I took hold of Julia's elbow and told her to come on.

Julia looked over her shoulder at Robert, who was going down to put the empty glasses on the bar-counter.

'Perhaps we'll have somewhere to live before then. Joe says you've been to some agents.'

Robert's answer was delivered weightily. 'I've been talking to some of my friends who know about these things.'

'Dear Robert, that's not very definite,' said Julia.

When Robert came back he behaved as if the exchange were over.

Julia looked up into his face, hesitated for a moment, and then smiled at him. She took hold of Robert's hand, and twisted her fingers through his while we walked down the corridor.

We went in to see *Love For Love*.

CHAPTER III

TALK BY THE FIRESIDE

Myrtle's sad and fearful prophesy of a desperately cold winter was being borne out. By the end of January we thought the weather had reached its bitterest, the snow its thickest and our fuel its shortest. Haxby had not got a job, and Robert was in bed with influenza. Dr Chubb, wearing his winter combinations and his galoshes, was an example to us all of what comes from taking every sensible precaution. He was cold, he was alarmed because the office was not heated properly, but he was clearly blooming with health. And he was in London all the time. I was at a loss to know why he was not on the second half of his tour of industries concerned in making the A 15 and the A 16, although both Robert and I were also at something of a loss to know what he had done on the first half. We had heard one or two surprising bits of gossip about his activities.

One afternoon Chubb came into my office and proposed to my surprise that we should go out for tea at his club.

'I don't think anybody can work with cold feet,' he said, giving me a nervous toothy smile. 'I know I can't.'

We got a taxi. I found that he belonged to one of the biggest, though hardly the most gentlemanly clubs in London. We were drawn through swing-doors into what looked like an American hotel, complete with tobacconist shop, bookstall, post-office and palm lounge. Dr Chubb suggested we wash our hands.

'I didn't wash before I left the office,' he said. 'I find cold water doesn't really cleanse one's hands properly. I don't know if you agree.'

The water in the wash-basins was only tepid. Dr Chubb was

dismayed.

We went into a huge lounge, where we saw a log fire burning brightly. We sat down in front of it, Chubb rubbing his hands with satisfaction. He ordered tea.

'This was a good idea,' I said, looking round me, admiringly.

'I'm glad you were able to come, because I've been wanting to have a little talk with you for some time.'

I glanced at him. He went on.

'But we're all so busy, that is to say, you and I are very busy, and of course Your Friend being only on part-time makes everything a bit more difficult...' He waited.

I pretended to think. A waiter placed a tray before us, with a pot of tea on it and some rounds of under-buttered toast. 'I expect you'd like me to officiate,' said Chubb, looking over the top of his spectacles.

I turned my attention to the room which was so big that the massive pieces of furniture seemed ordinary-sized. From the lofty ceiling hung dusty glass chandeliers in which every third bulb only was lit. Over the mantelpiece there was a mural painting whose subject I presumed to be allegorical since the swans appeared to be on an equal footing with the human beings. What interested me most was the smell of the place – I knew it was the long-standing scent of cigars, but had my nose been presented with it in other circumstances I could easily have taken it for a whiff of the stables.

Dr Chubb was talking to me. I just came in at the point where he was saying: ' – and I said to my wife I should like to read the novels you and Your Friend wrote, so she asked her library if they could get them for her.'

'Did they?' I said, really interested. Our books were out of print.

Chubb sipped his tea.

'Yes. They managed to get hold of them for us.'

'Have you read them?'

'Yes. I thought perhaps you'd like to hear what we thought about them – I may say that my wife reads a great deal, in fact she reads a great deal more than me, especially novels. I like a good biography myself, though I've read a great many novels in the past.' He began to spread some blackberry jelly on his toast. 'We enjoyed your novels and Your Friend's.'

'Excellent,' I said.

'I don't know if you'd like some of our further comments.'

'Delighted.' Nothing pleased me more than comments on my books, provided they were favourable.

Dr Chubb took another piece of toast. 'I'm afraid the tea here isn't as good as it used to be. Before the war it was quite different.'

'And the novels?' I said.

'Yes, yes.' Dr Chubb wiped his lips with his handkerchief, and pushed it back in his left cuff, leaving a point sticking out. He said:

'First of all, I think I may say that my wife preferred Your Friend's books to yours – '

'Women's books.'

' – Whereas I haven't really made up my mind, because I like to think things over a little longer before I commit myself. All the same I can see that yours were written, I don't know how to put it exactly, but perhaps I might say – seriously.'

'That's just it!'

Chubb went on. What he said was bumblingly pedestrian. Yet it seemed to me, in the light of his opening remark, sensible and perspicacious. I forgot that he had not brought me out to tea to give me a layman's literary criticism. I was flattered.

In rounding off his views Chubb came back to his original comment.

'Of course!' I said. 'You see I'm a serious writer.'

Chubb looked at me. He said:

'And I can see that Your Friend is, too.'

'Of course. We're both serious writers. It's the only thing we really care about.'

Chubb nodded encouragingly. 'I'm told he is on part-time so as to give himself more time for writing, but I should have thought writing was a full-time job.'

'It is! As soon as he gets a chance, he'll leave the government service like a shot. And I shall follow. Please God it won't be long now – six months at most!'

Chubb was silent. I had not been looking at him while I

made my speech. I now turned and saw him smiling at me over his spectacles. His eyes were brighter – and his cheeks pinker, with the radiance of a man's face when he has found out something he wanted to know. I could have kicked myself for telling him the truth: Robert would never have done it.

'I hope your estimate turns out to be correct.' His tone was full and amiable. He stood up and warmed his seat at the fire.

I watched him. Then I went to the fire and did the same. We stared round the room, at bald members having their tea. After a while he said:

'I don't think I shall go back to the office again.'

He jingled some keys in his pocket. His face looked both alert and relaxed. He was thinking, I had not the slightest doubt, that things were going very nicely.

CHAPTER IV

THE IMPORTANCE OF A SIGNATURE

I decided, after Chubb had set off for Waterloo in a taxi, that I would go back to the office after all. It was already quite dark outside, and as I trudged through the slush I wished I had Chubb's galoshes, old woman though they made him look.

I began to recall the bits of gossip we had heard about his tour. It sounded as if, in his bumbling pedestrian way, he was going much further than Robert and I towards expressing personal opinions on the A 16 controversy. I was puzzled.

In Trafalgar Square there was a trace of fog which gave the lamps a halo and diffused the pools of light on the unmelted snow. I tried to persuade myself the weather was slightly warmer.

On my desk I found a note from my personal assistant saying that Mr Froggatt wanted to see me. I rang for her.

'I told him I thought you'd gone to a meeting with Dr Chubb,' she said.

This seemed to me highly satisfactory: it came naturally to her to conceal my movements, in particular my absences from my desk.

I enquired if she had rung Robert's flat to see if he was better. An alarmed look crossed her plump, pretty face. I was reminded once again of how rarely a strong desire to please went with a talent for office method. I telephoned for Froggatt. He came in carrying a sheaf of papers.

'I was hoping to see you before the end of the afternoon, sir.' He came slowly to the end of his first period, and began the second as if he were making a fresh start. 'It's about the little matter of the Forms 404a/45.'

I pretended not to know what they were by their number. Froggatt took it with perfect ease.

'Will it help you to recall them, sir, if I remind you that they're the forms you suggested might be printed on a roll?'

'Impossible I could have said that, Froggatt. You've invented it yourself.'

Froggatt shook his head, and a faint smile crossed his long slightly bloodhound-like face. 'Ah no, sir, I'm afraid not. Not after a lifetime in the service.'

He put his sheaf of papers on my desk and remained standing. I told him to sit down. The papers were the 404a/45 forms for special reports. Froggatt said:

'You asked me to investigate a certain delay there was in 404a/45s going out. I have investigated that delay, and incidentally confirmed the idea I had in the first instance.' He paused. 'I'm afraid the delay occurred because they were in the hands of Dr Chubb, awaiting his signature.'

I said 'Dr Chubb!' in great astonishment. 'Why didn't you sign them yourself?'

Sir Francis had authorised Froggatt to sign them in the absence of Robert and me, so we always let him sign them. We thought he liked to see his signature go out in multiplicate.

'When Dr Chubb came to help the division in the matter of the A 15 and the A 16,' said Froggatt, 'he thought it proper for the signing of 404a/45s to revert to the former practice, of being signed by someone at his own level.'

Neither Robert nor I knew Chubb had taken it out of Froggatt's hands.

'He's been signing them all for some weeks past.' Froggatt had dropped his subfusc playfulness. 'Some evenings he's been here till seven o'clock.'

Froggatt was clearly not the only one who liked seeing his signature go out in multiplicate. To save him seeing my amusement I sent him away.

I was interested as well as amused by Chubb's latest manoeuvre. I did not see how or why it could reasonably be stopped. On the other hand, I saw no reason why he should not pay for it. With Froggatt's aid we might find him many many more documents on which to write his glorious name, and have him staying at the office till eight o'clock every night of the week to do it. Perhaps it might encourage him to go away on the rest of his tour.

CHAPTER V

ANOTHER MORNING BEFORE THE OFFICE

It was a dark morning, and I was rather late setting out for the office. When I came up the street I found Myrtle standing on the pavement outside the entrance.

'Darling, what on earth?' I began, and then saw her face more closely. She was desperately unhappy.

'I was waiting to see you.'

I put my arms round her. She looked up at me, her eyes wide and her features still.

'I've told him.'

'When?'

'Last night.'

'How did he take it?'

'Terribly.'

She turned her head away, and leaned against me as if she were exhausted.

I said: 'We can't stand here in the cold.' And I led her along. Instead of going into my office-building, I took her round the square towards a café facing the Houses of Parliament. From time to time I glanced at her, but she was silent. Her cheeks, just below the eyes, were bright and puffy from weeping.

'You'd better have some hot coffee.'

'I've had some.'

'Already?'

Myrtle turned to me with deep reproach. 'We've been up all night.'

I refrained from expostulating. We had come to the café, and I took her in. It was a bare slightly steamy room, with men sitting in their overcoats at marble-topped tables. Through the window, we could see between trays of cakes and rolls the shadows of vehicles moving towards Westminster Bridge.

I said: 'What decisions did you come to?'

Myrtle's shoulders relaxed and she sighed helplessly. 'We didn't decide anything.'

'Will he agree to a divorce?'

She did not reply.

A waitress came to our table, picked up the cruet, whisked the marble-top with a damp cloth, and set two cups of coffee before us. The coffee smelt good. Myrtle stretched her hand out shakily. I offered her a cigarette.

'How did it all happen?' I said.

'We've been staying in London for the last three days, while Dennis looked for a job.'

'Has he found one?'

'Yes.' Myrtle spoke as if it were something I might have expected had I been a bit more sensible. 'He's got a job at the BBC.'

I said mildly: 'As a disc-jockey?'

'No. In the News Room, of course.'

One of Myrtle's friends had lent her a flat, and it was there that the scene had taken place. On the evening of Haxby's getting a job, they had gone out to dinner, supposedly to celebrate. The celebration had fallen hopelessly flat.

'I tried to drink a lot, but it had no effect. He drank hardly anything. It was terrible. We both knew.'

I stared at her.

'He said: "I suppose this is where you're going to tell me!" '

Myrtle looked at me with her head slightly lowered. 'He'd known about us all the time.'

Immediately she said it I knew that it must be true and that it must have been obvious. We had been moderately discreet: I had never been near Myrtle's town or any of her friends whom Haxby knew. Yet it was absurd to think that in London we were isolated. The only thing that had isolated us was our own desire not to be observed when we were doing something we did not want people to see.

I said: 'Oh God.' The man had borne up well.

Myrtle said: 'I ought to have told him before.'

I did not say anything.

She burst out: 'I wish I hadn't told him now!'

I said: 'It had to be done, darling.' Across the table I took hold of her hand: it lay limply in mine.

To attain our own selfish desires we usually had to make someone else suffer, yet if we ourselves were not completely selfish the other person's suffering was bound to hurt us in return – I refrained from explaining this idea to Myrtle.

'I wish he weren't so helpless about it,' Myrtle said. 'If only he'd been angry and violent!'

I did not think this was very reasonable if she wanted him to give her a divorce.

She said: 'He started to weep.'

'What did you do?'

'I wept too.' She added: 'We made tea about six times.'

There was a pause. I signalled the waitress and ordered some more coffee. The number of people at the other tables had diminished. I noticed that the walls of the room were covered with a mosaic of dreary grey little stones. The coffee came, steaming.

I watched Myrtle. I wanted to know exactly how far she had got towards persuading Haxby to divorce her. I said:

'I suppose he realised what it would all lead to. I mean, that you wanted a divorce?'

'It took hours before I could get round to that. I don't know... There was so much emotion, I couldn't have believed it.' Myrtle glanced away. 'I suppose when you have been married to someone for years, it's like that. He knew all about it, and yet that didn't seem to make any difference. I had to tell him that we wanted to be married – he didn't seem to have grasped the fact.' She dropped her head, as if she were going to burst into tears. 'He told me I could come and live with you, if I wanted.'

I glanced at her, wondering if she was speaking the truth. I thought she was. I said:

'Does that mean he doesn't want to divorce you?'

'I don't think he believes it's possible.'

'But, darling – '

'He's been completely faithful to me all the time.'

Suddenly I realised there must still be a hope in Myrtle's mind that he would let her divorce him. It seemed to me incredible. Then it dawned on me that her alarm and distaste at being publicly pronounced the guilty party might well be the strongest emotion of all. The first miracle, of Haxby's not returning, had failed to happen. There was now a second miracle in view. I said:

'Darling, you can't hope that he'll let you divorce him. Anyway, I wouldn't ask him. Dammit, it wouldn't be fair.'

Myrtle said: 'You don't appear to care about me!'

'Of course I do.'

'If you did you couldn't accept it so easily.'

I was silent.

Myrtle's bitterness ebbed away. She looked at me affectionately. 'It's awfully hard for me, darling. I can't bear to think of people saying…' She did not finish the sentence. Her eyes filled with tears. 'I don't know how I could ever tell my father. The poor old man, it would break his heart.'

I was at a loss before an entirely new line. This was the first time her father had come into it. Myrtle and Haxby lived in his house, and he was quite fond of Haxby. He was a kindly, affectionate and, I thought, rather sly old man.

I said tritely: 'But he wants you to be happy.' I did not really believe it would break his heart.

'Yes,' said Myrtle, in a non-committal tone.

'I'm sure he does.'

'He's so dependent on me.' It was Myrtle's belief that her father loved her more than he loved her brother and her sister.

I felt that we were getting too far away from the point.

'One can't just leave people so easily,' Myrtle said.

Nevertheless her tone made me think she was recovering a little of her strength of purpose.

'You won't be seeing any less of your father,' I said. 'It's Dennis that you'll have to leave.' I took hold of her hand. 'I want you, too, darling, and you can't have both of us.'

Her fingers tightened in mine. Suddenly she burst out: 'Oh God!' I could see she had collapsed into great unhappiness again.

'What is it?'

'You don't realise what you're asking.' She paused in such a way that I was bound to say 'What?'

With great emotion Myrtle replied:

'*He says he can't live without me.*'

I looked down at my empty cup. By instinct I recognised something really menacing. It was something I could not say myself. It would have weighed with most women. It had weighed with Myrtle.

Myrtle was looking at me.

I shook my head and was silent.

At that moment we heard the clanging of a bell outside. It was a fire-engine going past. Everyone in the café sat up. We saw a dim flash of red through the window, and a waitress near the door ran out into the street to watch. I allowed the diversion to distract us altogether. I did not want to go on with the scene. I could see only danger in discussing who could live without whom. I shifted in my chair and said:

'I really must go to the office, darling.'

Myrtle quietly put on her gloves. I called the waitress and paid the bill. We walked out into the street. The grey sky was lit by a faint sunny gleam. We passed men shovelling snow from the gutters. Big Ben began to chime quarter to eleven. At the bottom of Whitehall we paused and arranged to meet again at lunchtime. I found Myrtle a taxi and she went away.

CHAPTER VI

CONFRONTATION AT NIGHT

O n the following day Myrtle went home, leaving Haxby in lodgings in London. Nothing was settled about the divorce. At the weekend she returned to stay with me.

Saturday was Julia's birthday and we were invited to dine at her flat. Myrtle decided to try and cheer herself up with a tot of whisky before we set out. She had some success, and when she met my landlady on the stairs she gave her an absurdly over-cordial, smirking 'Good evening, Mrs Burdup.'

Mrs Burdup addressed me. She had me on the hip. And she said: 'I was just coming up to tell you the boiler's broken down.' She looked me in the eye. 'So there won't be any hot water for baths tonight.'

It was quite false. She knew that I knew it was false. I did not say anything because I had been given a glimpse into the depths of her nature – her meanness was stronger than her ladylikeness.

When we were outside Myrtle said: 'Where's her husband? She doesn't look like a widow to me.'

'Left her on the wedding-night, I should think.'

'I wonder if he'll turn up again.'

I felt for Burdup. I thought he would only turn up again if he were insane. While I was thinking, Myrtle stopped a taxi. 'It's so cold,' she explained. And as she leaned her head on my shoulder inside the taxi, she said: 'If the snow doesn't go soon, I think I shall die.'

Myrtle's spirits rose when she found Julia's flat was warm. The set of pale green rooms were the warmest we had been in for weeks. Myrtle walked through them with delight. Julia followed her.

'It's very important to have a flat that's got really good

central-heating,' Julia said. Behind Myrtle's back she gave me a bright-eyed, knowing grin: 'It couldn't be more important.'

We went into the room where Julia had first entertained me. It looked different. I glanced round at the glossy paint, the satinwood writing-desk, the elegant small tables. There were flowers everywhere: I distinctly remembered that on the previous occasion there had been none. Robert was not the kind of man who gave women flowers. There were daffodils, roses, lilac. The girls were admiring each other's dresses – Julia's was black and she had two brilliant clips at the neck.

'Robert's given me these,' she was saying. She took the clips off, for Myrtle to see. I thought of the yellow sapphire.

'Robert has decided we're going to drink champagne in place of cocktails. He's going to start a new fashion.'

'Lovely,' said Myrtle, breathlessly.

More of Robert, I thought. Julia looked carefree and gay. It suddenly crossed my mind that they had chosen this evening to tell us they were going to get married.

Just then Robert arrived. He came into the room with a proprietorial air. He was wearing a beautiful new suit and a lustrous grey tie. Julia put her arm round his neck and led him to the ice-bucket. He opened one of the bottles of champagne and the party began.

I doubt if Julia was outstanding as a cook, but under the influence of champagne we thought she had made an excellent dinner. We ate with pleasure and gusto. The candle-light glowed on Julia's face and Myrtle's. The walls seemed further away and less green. The radiators poured out their warmth. We began to feel intimate, easy, united. Outside, there was cold and snow and hurrying disinterested people in the streets. Inside, everything was transformed. I thought we must all get married and go on having dinner-parties like this.

While Julia had gone out to make the coffee Myrtle put her hand softly in my lap. We looked into each other's eyes. Left to himself Robert poured the remainder of the champagne into his own glass and drank it. Julia brought in a tray with coffee-cups – as she leaned forward the candle-light glowed down her bosom. The smell of coffee wafted across to me.

'Isn't this wonderful!' I said.

And Julia, seeing me engaged with Myrtle, stood beside Robert and ran her fingers through his hair. We were all alight with amorousness.

At this moment we heard the click of a door. It was the front-door of the flat. Someone was coming in. We turned.

The dining-room door opened, a man looked in, as if by accident, and disappeared again.

We knew at once that it was Wladislaw.'

Neither Robert, Myrtle nor I could say anything. Julia called after him and ran out of the room. We stood up. From down the corridor came voices, Julia's harsh, the man's strong and nasal.

Julia was saying: 'I told you not to come back.'

'I didn't know you were here.'

'That's no excuse.'

'It's not supposed to be an excuse.'

'What have you come for?'

'To get some things from my room.'

We stopped listening for a moment. Robert said something, but I forget what it was. I no doubt replied. Our conversation was a formality.

We heard Wladislaw saying more loudly: 'I wish to speak with him.' Julia replied in a low voice that we could not catch. We heard them coming towards us. Julia appeared in the doorway, and said: 'Wladislaw wants to meet you. I'm going to introduce him.'

We saw Wladislaw standing behind her. Julia did not move. He stretched out his hand towards us but it was impossible for him to pass her in the doorway. He was not quite as tall as Julia but he was unusually broad.

'I beg your pardon,' he said politely, and stepped forward, so that he and Julia were wedged.

'Fool!' Julia whispered.

'I must apologise,' said Wladislaw to us, as if he were apologising for Julia. He turned to Julia to present him: 'Please.'

Julia introduced us in turn, and he shook hands. He was a very powerfully-built man, with a big torso and rather short legs. His neck was as wide as his face, and his muscles seemed to fill out his clothes. He looked about forty-five years old. He had close-cropped dark hair and small piercing grey eyes. By his face we knew immediately what Julia had not seen fit to tell us – that he was a highly intelligent man.

'I'm glad of this opportunity to meet you,' he said to Robert as he shook hands. He spoke English easily with a good accent. Then he turned to Julia. 'I should like coffee, please.'

There were only four chairs. We all filed along the corridor to the living-room, Wladislaw firmly and politely waiting till the last. Myrtle took hold of my hand and sat down beside me on the sofa. Robert and Wladislaw sat in armchairs facing each other, Robert in the armchair beside the telephone, Wladislaw near the piano – behind his head I noticed the photograph of the woman with ostrich plumes in her hair.

Julia gave us our coffee. Her face was tense and her eyes glittered. Provocatively she sat down on the arm of Robert's chair.

Wladislaw offered her his chair. She refused.

'Perhaps Mrs Haxby would like a cigarette,' he said. With a nervous irritated gesture, Julia handed Myrtle a box.

'I don't smoke, myself,' Wladislaw said to Myrtle. 'You know?'

Suddenly Julia turned to Robert and took hold of his arm. She said:

'Wladislaw hasn't been living here!'

There was silence.

'That is correct,' said Wladislaw.

'Robert will believe it without your corroboration.'

'Such a statement is better when corroborated.'

'If it's true it doesn't need corroboration.'

'No. People don't necessarily believe such a statement because it's true. They believe because it's corroborated.' He paused. 'Corroboration is the decisive factor.'

'Damn corroboration!' Julia was having difficulty in controlling herself. 'And don't stare at me like Svengali!'

Wladislaw jumped up from his chair.

'You're not tall enough!' Julia said.

Wladislaw sat down again.

Julia sipped her coffee triumphantly.

'I didn't know Svengali was tall,' said Myrtle. She laughed. 'I know he had a big black beard.'

I squeezed her hand to make her be quiet.

Robert said authoritatively: 'I should have thought it was a matter of presence, rather than of height or of beard.'

'Thank you,' said Wladislaw. 'That's what I thowt.' It was the first word I had heard him seriously mispronounce.

'Would you like a glass of champagne?' Myrtle said to him. I had a strong suspicion she found him attractive.

Wladislaw glanced at Julia. 'I would like some brandy.' He had noticed four balloon glasses standing on the writing-desk.

Julia had to go and fetch another glass. She poured out brandies for all of us, and handed them round. While she was doing it, Wladislaw addressed himself to Robert.

'I wish to explain why I came here tonight.'

Julia stopped to look at him. 'You didn't come to collect something?'

'Yes. That was true. I came also because I was hoping to find *him* here.' He drank a little brandy, put down the glass, and sat with his fists resting on his massive thighs. Julia, instead of sitting down, stood by the fireplace, which was glowing with an electric imitation coal-fire.

'I wanted to meet you,' Wladislaw said to Robert. 'I told Julia it's very important.' He paused. 'I asked her to arrange, but she refused.'

'Of course I refused!' Julia's eyes suddenly flashed with amusement. 'As I knew he was proposing to tell you I'm either a dipsomaniac or a nymphomaniac.'

'That's not true!' Wladislaw turned to her with startling violence.

'Of course it is!' Julia laughed at him openly. She sipped her brandy and her hair fell forward over her cheeks.

'That's not true!' His voice was louder.

Robert intervened. 'What did you want to say to me?'

Wladislaw turned back to Robert. 'I will tell you.' He was startlingly polite again. I wondered if he had been drinking before he came in. For several moments he looked at Robert with a fixed expression. He said: 'I believe you wish to make Julia happy.'

Robert nodded his head gravely and did not speak. He gave the impression that the occasion was too grave for speech.

Wladislaw said: 'It's very difficult. You know?'

Robert watched him with bright eyes.

'She is very difficult woman to understand,' Wladislaw said. 'You know?'

'I do know.'

Wladislaw paused. He was perfectly sober. He gave Robert a particularly piercing look:

'It's only one who understands her who can make her happy.'

I could tell it was his great point. He must have made it many times before. Instantly Julia cried:

'I deny that!'

Robert and Wladislaw glanced at each other. Robert said with enormous weight:

'I agree with you.'

Wladislaw was deeply impressed.

'I don't know,' said Robert, 'if anyone can make her permanently happy.' He shook his head, as God might while thinking of the human race.

'I have tried to understand her,' Wladislaw said.

'I try to use such insight as I have,' said Robert.

'I can tell you have insight,' said Wladislaw, looking into his eyes unwaveringly. 'I can judge a man's face.'

There was an impressive pause. Julia said with sudden amusement: 'I can't see where you two go from there.'

Wladislaw said to Robert with powerful logic:

'Can you make her happy temporarily?

Robert of course did not reply.

'I am a simple man, as you see. And so I ask you, can you offer the things she needs?' Wladislaw made a sweeping gesture with his hand. 'I bowt this flat, these flowers, these beautiful things.' He paused. 'But that's not all, to make her happy. You know?'

Julia said: 'He does know,' and drained her glass.

Wladislaw looked at her. 'You see,' he said. 'She drinks too much.'

'What did I tell you?' said Julia to Robert.

'When I am not here,' Wladislaw said, 'she drinks too much. When I am not here she sees too many men.' He was watching her all the time.

'Dipso *and* nympho!' Julia laughed gleefully. She poured herself some more brandy.

'Too many men are bad for her,' Wladislaw said loudly. He stood up.

Julia said: 'Dear Wladislaw, when will you understand I'm not the Penelope type?' She appealed to Robert: 'Can't you explain to him?'

Wladislaw said: 'No, she is not the Penelope type.'

We all turned to Julia. I cannot say that she looked like Penelope. Wladislaw said:

'She needs a man who will look after her all the time. She needs a man who will be always vigilant.' He spoke with great emotion, his eyes fixed on her fascinatedly. 'She needs a nurse. I am that man.'

'You, a nurse?' said Julia. 'You'd be dismissed the first day.'

Wladislaw was angered. 'Don't say that!'

'I won't listen to you saying you want to nurse me. I know what you want.'

'Don't provoke me! I am trying to be fair to you.'

'Fair to me!' A reddish colour rose up in Julia's neck. 'You call that fair?'

Wladislaw suddenly faced her. When he stood close to her his eyes looked hotter. 'For three years I have tried to understand your weakness and your foolishness. You know what I have to bear. You know how many times I have to forgive you – '

'I didn't ask you to forgive me!'

'You know how many lovers – '

'Stop!' Julia shouted.

'I will go on.'

'Go on, then!'

'He should know what you are like!'

'I've told him everything!'

'You are lying!'

Julia flung her brandy into his face.

For a moment Wladislaw was blinded. Then as if he had not

noticed it he went nearer to Julia. His face was close to hers. His voice trumpeted violently.

'You know what you will become if I am not here to look after you? You will be in a home for drunkards! You will be on the streets!'

Julia moved her face closer to his. 'But not *yet*!' She suddenly broke into high-pitched laughter. 'You talk as if it were all going to happen *tomorrow*!'

Wladislaw seized her. Passionate rage seemed to have brought to them the pitch of incandescence. Myrtle cried out with alarm.

Julia heard Myrtle. She tried to wrench herself free from Wladislaw. 'Stop him!'

Instantly we all jumped to our feet. There was a moment's silence. And there was another strange noise – from Robert. He was standing motionless.

'Sorry,' he said. 'Pins and needles in my leg.'

Wladislaw let go Julia. He went to Robert to support him. The rest of us watched. Even months afterwards I found it impossible to convince Myrtle and Julia that Robert was not shamming. Robert stamped his foot a few times. Wladislaw solicitously offered him brandy.

'Thank you,' said Robert. 'I'm all right.' He limped into the middle of the group. He paused. 'I think it's time we went home.'

Wladislaw was looking at Julia. He wiped the back of his hand across his face.

'I'm not staying here,' Julia said. 'Robert, take me with you!'

'Do you mean that?' Wladislaw was staring at her with desire. He could not conceal it.

'I'm not staying here!' Julia was watching him, her eyes brilliant.

We were all silent.

'Robert!' Julia put her hand on Robert's arm. 'Please, take me away from here now!'

Wladislaw was watching him. Gravely Robert nodded.

That night Julia stayed in Robert's flat.

CHAPTER VII

'SHALL I MARRY HER?'

Julia stayed only one night in Robert's flat. In the early hours of the morning Wladislaw rang her up to apologise for making a scene and to say that he was moving out of her flat never to return. Although Julia did not believe a word of it, Robert persuaded her to go home again.

Myrtle said to me: 'Darling, why doesn't Robert let Julia stay in his flat?'

It was a difficult question to answer. Robert was not troubled by the interventions of a Mrs Burdup, which Myrtle could understand; nor was he short of money, as I was. I told Myrtle I did not know, this being simpler than trying to explain Robert's over-riding dislike of being given no option.

Myrtle said nothing more. She seemed altogether subdued since the party, chastened and discouraged. I fancied she recollected it as an unpleasing revelation for which I was responsible.

Robert seemed unperturbed. From instinct I assumed that he must really have made up his mind what he was going to do. He watched the events that followed with lively absorbed interest.

The first thing was a long letter from Wladislaw to Julia, withdrawing his love and offering in its place his friendship.

'What does Julia think of that?' I asked.

'I'm afraid she regards it quite simply as another way of trying to get into bed with her.'

'It is,' I said.

'It is,' said Robert.

Out of friendship Wladislaw proposed to go on paying the rent of Julia's flat till the end of the month. It was at this point that Robert discovered a fact which Julia, for all her worldliness and determination, had never got clear. Wladislaw was quite rich. He was not a White refugee. His family had since long before the war had business connections in England. Wladislaw had been to an English public-school – that was why he spoke the language so well. And he now made a substantial income in the City.

The letter ended with an expression of Wladislaw's great respect for Robert and desire to meet him again.

Robert met him one lunch-time and came back to report on it. Wladislaw was most anxious to prove that his feeling for Julia was no more than friendship. To that end he wanted to do something to help Julia, in particular to get her away from her present circle of friends whom he felt were responsible for her moral decline. He proposed to finance her going up to Cambridge to read for a degree.

I was staggered by the idea of planting Julia among seven thousand young men.

'Hasn't he thought of that?' I said.

Robert shook his head. 'He's thinking of her education.'

'And Julia?'

'She's thought of the fact to which you refer.' He smiled: 'She wouldn't go, anyway.'

Wladislaw continued to press the claims of his friendship in other different forms. Unhappily it appeared that also he was employing private detectives to watch Julia's flat. Somehow it did not remind either Robert or me of the jealousy we had felt over The Headlamps and My Last One. Wladislaw gave us a glimpse of a passion more sustained, more obsessive and more active than anything we had ever felt.

One morning Robert came into my office shortly after I had arrived. His face was pale, and his eyes were sparkling with what I thought was suppressed amusement.

To my surprise he began asking me if I had heard from Myrtle. I had received a short unsatisfactory note. Robert stood in his overcoat by the window, as if he were interested in looking through the opaque windows into the empty well of the building. I could not tell if he was listening.

Suddenly he came and sat on the corner of my desk. He took

out Myrtle's ivory cigarette-holder and lit a cigarette. Then he glanced at me.

'Look here,' he said. 'Reticent man though I am, I can't help telling you what happened last night. It was an incident simply made for you.'

I pulled out a drawer and put my feet up.

'I was at Julia's,' Robert said. 'We'd been drinking after dinner. It was about half past eleven and we'd just got to bed. In fact I'd just' – he found it impossible to say what he had just, and went on – 'when the telephone beside the bed rang. Julia picked it up, and Wladislaw's voice said resonantly: "Don't do it, Julia! Don't do it!"'

Robert took off his overcoat, and pulled up a chair beside mine. His amusement died away. After a few minutes I realised that his mood had changed to completely serious. He smoked in silence, with his head bent. I waited for him to speak to me.

At last he said: 'Ought I to marry this girl?'

I stared at him and could find no reply.

'I expect you realise I've been pretty near to it,' he said.

I nodded.

'She's closer than you think to my line.'

'I know that.'

I saw him look at me with interest. His line was The Headlamps – a lost soul, who made him suffer for loving her. I saw Julia in the same rôle. It made no difference that The Headlamps slept with nobody and Julia with everybody. The line, as he called it, could be the same. It could be the same in his loving her, and the same in his having to suffer for it.

He said: 'It's clear that she needs me.' He paused. 'She needs me more than I need her.'

I moved my feet and the drawer creaked just as he said something else. It sounded like 'That's the trouble' but I did not catch it.

CHAPTER VIII

A TOOTHY MACHIAVELLI

Dr Chubb had still not left London for the second half of his industrial tour. I grew steadily more puzzled.

We had tried to check the stories about his indiscreet expressions of opinion on his first tour. They were absurdly conflicting – some people said he had told them they could go on making A 15s indefinitely; others, equally trustworthy, that he had hinted at something new coming along which would oust the A 15 within a year.

'Do you think he's trying to prove his impartiality?' said Robert.

I took the rumours more seriously. Chubb might conceivably have suspected his task was designed by Robert for the dual purpose of getting him out of the way and putting him in a position to make a blunder. But there was no reason why he should go in for fantastic behaviour.

From time to time I passed Chubb going down the corridor to wash his hands. He invariably complained that office-work was preventing him from travelling.

One evening Froggatt had been consulting me just before it was time to go home. I was sitting tiredly at my desk, and I tried to cheer Froggatt and myself by saying the day's work was over.

'It may be for you,' said Froggatt: 'I've no doubt it is. Unfortunately I am not in that happy position.' The bloodhound-like lines below his eyes sagged. He waited for me to ask why, and then said: 'I now have to look forward to another hour's consultation with Dr Chubb.' He saw my astonishment. 'Yes, sir. It's becoming quite a regular feature.'

I straightened up. 'Don't go, for a moment.'

Froggatt waited respectfully. He said: 'I hope you don't think I'm offering a complaint. These consultations are necessary, I can assure you. And Dr Chubb is busy throughout the day.' He gave me a peculiar half-smile. 'He knows that he can always send for me when I'm just about to go home.'

It was not difficult to find out what was happening. Dr Chubb felt it was only proper that all the duties as well as document-signing, which Robert and I had delegated to Froggatt – for want of time, of course – should go to him, Chubb.

'I'm sure it's a great relief to me that they should.' Froggatt paused. 'However, at the moment Dr Chubb does not feel confident to carry them out independently. He discusses them all with me before he makes his decisions. I'm afraid it takes up more time than ever, that way.'

Robert was extremely adept at delegation, I was practising it assiduously, and we both had great confidence in Froggatt. Chubb had been quick in the uptake.

'In addition to this,' Froggatt continued, 'Dr Chubb has undertaken various other responsibilities. For example, he suggested to D.O.R.R.S. that he should attend the fortnightly conferences with Mr Irskine on staff matters.'

'Staff?' It was too much. 'Good God!'

'Certainly,' said Froggatt. 'I'm busy preparing a detailed report on the present staffing position for Dr Chubb at this moment.'

As soon as Froggatt left me, I went to Robert's office.

Robert was sitting at his desk, writing a memorandum to Sir Francis.

I sat down and waited till he had finished. He stood up. 'Ready?' He thought we were going home.

I shook my head. He sat on the edge of the table while I told him about Chubb's latest gambit. He listened, and then went to his telephone and rang up Chubb.

'Lunn tells me you'd like to see me,' he said. 'Would you come in now?'

A few moments later Chubb came in looking a trifle flustered. 'I did want to see you about certain matters.' He cast a hare-eyed look in my direction. 'But I don't recall mentioning it to Lunn.'

Robert smiled at him genially.

After a long preamble, Chubb settled down to work on something that was of no great importance and on which Froggatt could perfectly well have advised him. Robert listened patiently. When it was ending, Robert began to lead him round to the new and onerous activities that kept him from his travels.

Chubb looked worried. Comparing our division with the department from which he had come, Chubb felt that our administration and execution left much for him at least to desire.

'There's a certain lack of integration, if you know what I mean,' he said. 'Largely, I think, because it lacks a person whose responsibility it is to be responsible for that integration.'

I thought, somewhat irrelevantly: 'There's a lack of integration about what you say to the firms about the A 15 and the A 16, not to mention your efforts to get a better job.'

'That's most interesting,' said Robert, considerately. 'Perhaps we might discuss it some evening at greater length. Perhaps you'd put down a few points on paper.'

Chubb was encouraged. He went on to discuss staff. His worried look returned. We heard about the long hours he was forced to work, about the vast amount of detail in which a highly detailed report on the A 16 position had involved him, and above all about the responsibility. His cheeks grew ruddier and his eyes more anxious-looking.

'And I don't care to think of the position in due course,' he ended up.

'In due course?' Robert said, mildly.

Chubb could not resist saying, with nervous hesitation, 'I hear from Lunn that the department will not be able to count on your services for an indefinite period.' He stammered slightly. 'I don't know if I've understood the position correctly.' And he looked at Robert. 'I heard you were going to leave this place.'

The longer he went on looking at Robert, the more hare-eyed he became, because Robert said nothing at all.

CHAPTER IX

THE JAPANESE EMPEROR

A couple of days later James Irskine asked me to give him a game of squash. I wondered what was in the wind this time, and felt bored by the prospect of discussing it with him. The conversation began as soon as the game was over. The changing-room was quite empty, and I thought if he wanted to talk about A 15s he could. I sat down on a bench against the wall and began putting my racquet in its press. James did not sit down. He stripped, picked up a towel, and to my surprise appeared to be making for the showers. It was only a feint – he sat down beside me and said:

'How are you getting on with Chubb?' He bent his tall handsome head as if he were studying his toes.

I wondered if James could have been hearing the gossip we had heard. I said I had not seen much of Chubb.

'More than you expected.' He got a note of irony into his tone.

I said: 'He's got to go on tour soon. He's behind.'

'He's made a damned nuisance of himself here.'

I hesitated, and then realised James could not be referring to the rumours. The fact was that Chubb had been attempting to cultivate James's favour. It was an impossible task. James had no favour. On the other hand James was capable of making an alliance, and I had suspected Chubb was not doing badly. Somehow they had avoided a head-on collision over correct procedure.

I beckoned one of the attendants to bring us drinks.

'On the other hand,' James said, 'he's not a fool.' He glanced at me. 'He's just going to put in a report on staffing for Old Frank's reorganisation committee. It's not bad.'

As Chubb had discussed his report daily with James before putting it in, the opinion came to me as no surprise.

'I've got the draft, if you'd like to have a look at it.' James stood up and took down his jacket from the hook. 'Here it is.' He gave me two folded sheets of foolscap, tied his towel round his waist and went to the showers.

I read Chubb's report. It was not bad.

I cannot pretend that the methods of Robert and me were not a trifle rough-and-ready. Nobody could have done our job better than Robert: the Permanent Secretary knew it, Sir Francis knew it, everybody knew it. But it could have been done more properly. There is not the slightest doubt that had Robert and I been giving it our entire attention, we might have done it slightly differently. This was what Chubb knew.

So when I say Chubb's report was not bad, I mean that it made some just points. Chubb, with his own particular brand of departmental illiteracy, talked about the need for greater integration. What he meant was that it would have been proper for a man in Robert's position to busy himself continually with rather more things than Robert found time for, and that his instinct for propriety told him this was a serious defect in the organisation.

You may ask – 'If the job was being done as well as it could be done, what does it matter about its being done properly?' I can see that you are not a professional civil servant like Dr Chubb or James Irskine.

Chubb had a remedy for the defect. It was to create a post for a full-time senior person, whom Robert, as long as he remained, could advise, and who, when Robert left, would take over all responsibility. And if you think Chubb gave the faintest hint of who would be the most suitable man for this post, you have not begun to understand men of affairs.

James came back from the showers after an unusually short lapse of time.

'What do you think of it?'

'I'm interested.'

James put his foot on the bench beside me and dried his calf. It was clear to me that he would support Chubb's proposal, not because he thought anything of Chubb, not because he thought he would get the job – his next promotion would be to another department altogether. James would support it because it appealed to his clear machine-like concept of how things ought to be run.

I wondered whether the moment had come to tell James that Chubb was improperly committing himself to public, though contradictory, opinions on the A 16. I decided not.

I handed the papers back to James. Then I went to the showers thinking that Robert, if he did not want to find himself being placed on a handsome stately shelf, had got to turn his mind to office intrigue.

When the situation was presented to him Robert was of the same opinion. There was a meeting about staff a couple of days later, and Robert saw fit to attend. He came back with sparkling eyes. The office was going to run on its present lines till Robert left. Sir Francis, hypnotised by Robert's warnings of all sorts of contingencies, had put down Chubb's plan for the time being. There was nothing, as Robert knew, more liable to hypnotise Sir Francis than contingencies. I felt almost sorry for Chubb, a moderately sensible man being made to look stupid.

This scene was taking place in Robert's office. He took down his overcoat from the hat-stand, and bundled it on with great determination. I had recently seen him roused to activity by his private affairs: it was a long time since I had seen him roused over his career in the government service. I sensed that under his mischievous sparkle there was real anger.

'I'm damned if I'll be relegated,' Robert said, 'like a mediaeval Japanese emperor. I refuse to be the Late-Emperor to the Present-Emperor of Chubb.'

I reflected that there was no respite for a man of affairs.

'I told Old Frank I don't intend to go until I've seen the division though its main post-war problems. That gave them something to think about.' Robert paused. 'After that I hope there won't be a job for anybody. Chubb's only got five years to go.'

I picked up my hat from the table and put it on. We went down the corridor together. Chubb's office was in darkness. Robert cocked his thumb at the door.

'You can take it he'll be setting off on the second half of his tour next week at the latest.'

Robert sometimes observed to me that like women and elephants he never forgot. I knew that he would not forget Chubb. What was he going to do? Like most men of action Robert acted not by plan but by instinct. Chubb's downfall was at the back of his mind. Something would happen by chance. Instinct would tell him this was the moment. Then he would act.

CHAPTER X

IN A PUBLIC-HOUSE

There was a long silence from Myrtle. I thought it was time I asked Robert's advice.

'I'm getting nowhere.'

Robert said: 'I'm afraid you lack the touch for this kind of situation.'

I could see that as usual my asking for advice was merely going to produce discouraging home-truths about myself. Robert surveyed me with detachment.

'You don't give the air of suffering,' he said.

'I hope I don't,' I said, huffily. 'It's repellent.'

'It's very useful sometimes.'

'Hypocrite!'

Robert's lips tightened. 'Perfectly genuine.'

'There's no need to parade about in sackcloth and ashes.'

'It's not a bad thing. It makes people realise you're serious. People are very simple.'

He was talking sense – I disliked it.

'I believe in a stiff upper lip,' I said. You may think it a remarkable statement: it was true none the less.

Robert shrugged his shoulders. I could not help being somewhat borne down by logic. At last I said:

'What do you propose I should do?'

'Give an air of suffering.'

'How?'

'Don't ask me.'

I thought it over. It was an intolerable prospect. I said:

'I simply can't say I can't live without her.'

Robert said impatiently: 'Why not?'

'If moral weakness didn't blind you, you'd see it was

because it isn't the truth.' I looked at him. 'My Last One taught me that finally. I can't die for love.'

Robert put on a grave hollow tone. 'There are deeper truths than mere verbal statements.'

'Well,' I said, after thinking it over, 'if I do say it, I won't stay up all night to do it.'

'Please yourself,' said Robert.

'None of it pleases me at all!'

Robert shrugged his shoulders again. The conversation lapsed, but he was worried on my behalf. His apprehensions were more reliable than mine. I began to feel much more worried myself.

Next time Myrtle came up to London she said she had only time for a drink with me. Though all night was too long for showing an air of suffering, I was afraid a couple of hours might be too short. We arranged to meet in Piccadilly Circus and I arrived first. There was some sign of the weather changing, a new rawness and a faint humid warmth that made one dream of a thaw. All the same it was cold, and I began to stamp my feet and pace briskly to and fro. I realised I was making a mistake right at the start. A man who is suffering does not stamp his feet and flap his arms. He just lets himself freeze. I stopped immediately, and was feeling miserably cold when a taxi drew up and Myrtle got out.

I kissed her half-heartedly.

'Where are we going, darling?' she said.

I shook my head. 'I don't know.'

This was quite new to Myrtle. I always tried to have some convenient or attractive plan. She looked at me with surprise and interest. I was distinctly encouraged.

We began to walk along Piccadilly. It was evening, and the lights were just being switched off in the shop-windows.

'Any pub will do,' I said, taking care not to notice those we were passing though they were all familiar to me.

'Yes, darling,' said Myrtle in a subdued and puzzled tone.

I decided I was probably on the right lines. I had thought it over very carefully.

When I gave Myrtle the impression that I did not care which public-house we went to and did not even notice those we were passing, she knew at once that I had something on my mind. A horrifying corollary struck me – had she throughout all my years of observation, reflection and comment on this and that, thought I had nothing on my mind? I nearly stepped under a taxi.

'Darling!' Myrtle pulled me back.

I looked at her mutely.

'I think there's a pub up there,' she said. I signified that I might be led to it.

The public-house had not been open long, and it was almost empty. It was cold and rather cheerless. We were faced with a narrow alley and a line of tall uncomfortable wooden stools. We sat down. The floor was made of plain boards. I realised that Myrtle had brought me into the public bar.

In the ordinary way I should have moved her over to the saloon in fifteen seconds. That would have been fatal. I sat quite still and asked her distantly what she would like to drink. I looked down at the brown polished deal of the bar-top.

The drinks were put before us, and I realised that I had now got to begin. What was I to say? Something told me that I had got a chance of impressing her in a different way. The atmosphere was right. Now was the time when I must fight for her, and fight for her after a fashion she understood – that is to say not my own fashion but hers. What must I say?

'I can't live without you.'

My heart sank.

What then?

I drew in my breath slowly and then gave a long loud sigh.

'I'm terribly unhappy,' I said.

Myrtle looked at me. I think she saw that I was. Tears came up into her eyes.

If only I could have said 'I can't live without you!' I let my chin rest on my neck-tie and was silent.

We were quite alone on our side of the bar. There were people on the saloon side, but it was difficult to see them, because above the counter there was a structure consisting of a set of small windows, like ventilators, at head-height. You addressed the barman obliquely through the windows: below them you had a view, across the bar, of the chests and diaphragms of people in the saloon, just as presumably they had a view of yours. It was not the sort of view one would choose. I felt slightly sick with emotion. After a long time I said: 'This waiting is getting me down.'

Myrtle made some consoling remark.

I had an idea – I was certain I must state my case in familiar language. I simply must say things she could recognise. I let several minutes elapse and then made myself say: 'I want to be certain of you.'

Myrtle took hold of my hand, warmly. 'I know, darling,' she said.

The conversation was satisfactorily started. The remarkable thing was the length of time between the individual remarks. It seemed to be taking hours. But then how can one take an impressive length of time to say 'I am suffering'? I thought of saying it in other languages. 'Que je souffre!' – or would it be more French to say 'Qu'on souffre!'? Recollecting scenes from Dostoievsky, I thought that if only I knew the language, Russian would be just the ticket for me.

In the meantime, though I imagined I was being successful, I could not help feeling ashamed of myself. All my remarks were true, but they sounded deplorably pedestrian. Anybody could have said what I was saying. That was the point of it, but it made it no more appealing. To my way of thinking what made conversation worth having, what made any human activity worth doing, was the streak in it of originality, of creative art. But what of a streak in it of originality, of creative art, when conveying to a woman that you love her and want her to marry you? Ruinous! Pedestrian though my speeches were, pedestrian they had got to stay.

'I can't sleep.'

That was quite a good speech as well as true. 'Nor can I,' said Myrtle, but I knew I had gained through getting it in first.

It took me a long time to find the next one, and at the last minute I rejected it. 'I can't think of writing anything.' For me this meant great anguish, but I had a dreadful fear that Myrtle might feel it really to be all to the good. So I kept mum for another forty-five seconds – and if you try forty-five seconds by your watch you will find it a surprisingly long time.

I began to speculate on how many seconds had elapsed to ease the strain of preventing myself from saying something.

Suddenly I realised that Myrtle had spoken, had asked me something of transcending importance. She was looking at me with naif, shrewd, penetrating enquiry. She had said:

'Why do you want to marry me, darling?'

I had a choking sensation. I did not reply. More seconds passed, and a stream of reflections fled through my mind. Why did most men marry? Why had most of my friends married? Because they wanted a home, children, somebody to look after them, a regular mate – even the last was not the most important to a lot of them. They married so as to fit easily into society. Oh dear! I looked at Myrtle. Her round hazel eyes were fixed on me, with a serious, intent, trembling look.

It was the moment everything we had been saying had led up to: it was the moment I had come for. She was waiting to hear me say I could not live without her, waiting determinedly with deep emotion. I could not say it. With unexpected insight I knew it was not truthfulness that prevented me – I could have lied to her as most men would. It was pride. I would not bend my will an inch to hers, even to get something I wanted.

I muttered something incoherent. I felt I had the rest of my life in my hands. I really was suffering. And I could not help noticing how farcical it was.

I managed to say clearly what I had been muttering.

'Life seems utterly useless . . .'

It was as far as I could go. Was it far enough? I wondered. Oh, would it do?

There was a long pause. Myrtle put her hand on mine. She sighed. The critical moment had passed. Her fingers tightened. I looked up at her face. I was so uncertain of myself that I could not read anything in it.

'Darling,' she said.

That night, when I was at home in my flat, Robert rang me up.

'It's all right, old boy.'

'Is it? Are you really sure?'

'Myrtle rang me up immediately after she'd left you. She was genuinely alarmed. And upset.' Robert paused. 'She wanted to know what she could do to restore you.'

'What did you say?'

'Marry you as soon as possible.'

For a moment I could not speak.

Robert's tone changed. 'What *did* you say to her?'

CHAPTER XI

LOVE AND RENT

The following Saturday afternoon I met Julia by chance walking along the Chelsea embankment. We were both alone.

It was a charming afternoon. The thaw had come at last. It seemed as if there was water rushing in all directions – the river was flooding, gutters and spouts were gurgling, and rivulets were everywhere trickling down tree-trunks, railings, lamp-posts and walls. The sky was low and opalescent, and in its milky fawn light the last remnants of snow on the roof-tops shone like newly-cut lead.

I was standing beside the railings, idly watching the sights of the river. It was very quiet. On the opposite bank all the cranes and derricks were motionless. There was a single string of lighters coming up from the Pool, with only one of the crew to be seen, sitting on a hatch peeling potatoes over a bucket. Sounds of voices made me notice a group of Sea-scouts, standing on a flight of stone steps, waiting to embark for the weekend. Then a police launch went by, with a small red lamp flashing on top of the cabin. I was just contemplating my present affairs and wondering if I might not have done better in a sea-faring career, when I heard light vigorous footsteps.

It was Julia. She was looking very pretty, swinging along in a smart grey flannel suit, a little dachshund running at her heels.

'I'm in tremendously high spirits,' she said. 'Today's my day of liberation!'

'Please translate that into my language, Julia dear.'

'Today the occupation comes to an end.' She grinned at me furtively: 'Wladislaw moves out of my life for good.'

'I'm delighted. Are you sure of it?'

'Certain.' She glanced at me. 'I suppose you know he gave up offering me his love – I refused to accept it, anyway. So he consoles himself with the offer of his friendship. It doesn't appear to need requiting in the same way.'

'Oh, doesn't it!' I cried.

'He says definitely not.' Julia's mouth curled ironically. 'As a friend he stops paying the rent of my flat. So you see...'

'Distinctly unfriendly, I call that.'

'He offered to, but I'm not going to put myself under any more obligations to him.'

'What does that mean?'

'I'm not going to let him pay my rent.'

'Then who is going to pay it?' The ungentlemanly, if sensible, question slipped out.

At that moment the little dog ran a few yards away from her, and Julia was able to ignore my question by calling to it. We began to stroll along together.

I computed that Julia, as secretary of her Anglo-Polish society, could pay about a quarter of her upkeep.

Suddenly Julia said: 'I'm going to tell you, Joe, I simply can't keep it to myself.' She paused, and her voice, though it sounded softer, was undisguisedly triumphant. 'Robert's going to pay it.'

I said warmly: 'I'm glad.'

Julia was watching me out of the corner of her eye. 'Are you really?' Suddenly she took hold of my hand. 'You know I've always felt you were my only ally, Joe.'

'The only one?'

'Everybody else has tried to prevent me marrying Robert.'

I was silent, because I knew there was a good deal of truth in what she said. All the women in Robert's acquaintance thought it would be utterly, unmitigatedly wrong for him to marry Julia, and most of the men were doubtful. I squeezed her hand.

'You've been sweet to me, Joe,' said Julia.

'At least,' I said, 'I haven't expressed moral disapproval of you.'

'You can't imagine how happy it's made me – that Robert's

going to do it.' She turned to look at me. 'You don't know what a relief it is to a woman, to feel she's being kept.'

'Really?' I said, thinking ruefully of Myrtle.

Julia went on, her voice becoming warmer and deeper with hope: 'I think Robert's bound to marry me now.'

I forgot my own preoccupations in surprise. Could she really think that?

Julia loosed my hand. 'I can't decide whether it's the best idea for us to live together – I mean, before we get married . . .

'I simply couldn't tell you.'

Julia said, as if she were coming to the conclusion at the moment: 'I think I'll persuade him to move in straight away.' Her tone gave away that she had reached this conclusion long ago. 'Will you help me to persuade him?'

'I've never persuaded Robert to do anything, in my life.'

Julia looked at me disbelievingly.

I suddenly thought of Myrtle. I had never persuaded her to do much either. Robert and Myrtle were alike, in that what they were deciding to do always seemed mysterious and out-of-range. The activities of Julia's will and mine were somehow near the surface, of Robert's and Myrtle's deeply subterranean. No wonder Julia and I were the ones who got the worst of it.

'It's only possible to persuade Robert to do what he wants to do,' I said.

As usual, when I enunciated a truth about Robert's temperament, I was promptly denounced for it. Julia rounded on me.

'That's a confession of weakness!'

'Well!' I said, nonplussed.

'I can see now why you don't force Myrtle to marry you.'

'She can't bring herself to tell her father, because it will upset him,' I said. 'He's just had some kind of minor seizure . . .' I paused. 'All I can tell you,' I said, pulling myself together again, 'is that being strong doesn't happen to make the slightest difference.'

Julia checked herself, and became thoughtful. We walked along slowly. 'There must be something in what you say.' She glanced at me. 'I find it hard to understand. But you're never as wrong as all that.'

I bowed. 'Never let it be said I don't know how to accept a compliment.'

Julia's eyes sparkled with amusement. We had reached a bridge, and had to wait for the traffic. As we stood on the edge of the pavement, Julia said:

'I believe that at bottom Robert does want to marry me.' She paused. 'So you can go to work on persuading him.'

I looked at her. The soft opal light made her skin look clear and unlined. Her hair was brightly silky, and her eyes were shining. I should have liked to kiss her. She was happy.

'All right.' I held out my hand, and Julia took it.

'He's coming to dinner with me tonight, and I know he's having a drink with you first. Be my ally, Joe.' She squeezed my hand.

I looked into her eyes. 'Women are devil-bitches,' I said. And I swear that as I spoke she moved her face closer to mine. I kissed her on the mouth.

'H'm,' I said.

'Yes,' said Julia.

We parted, and I went back towards my flat. On the way I tried to piece out what was happening. I looked forward to my drink with Robert, and arrived punctually at his club.

Robert took me into the small room with windows along two sides, where we usually went. There was a whiskery old man dozing in one of the chairs, the same old man – immediately it took me back to an evening when the windows were filled with lemon-coloured bands of light and Robert first told me Julia wanted him to marry her. The tatty newspapers on the centre table, the absence of servants, and a feeling of nervous excitement. While Robert rang for the waiter and ordered sherry, I glanced into Pall Mall. It was dark and, in contrast to the light walls beside the window, the damp haze outside had a bluish tinge.

Robert and I sat side by side with a dim little table-lamp between us. We talked first of all about some of our friends in Oxford who had suffered an absurd defeat in College politics, then about Myrtle and Haxby, and finally about Julia. Robert ordered some more sherry. I told him that I had seen Julia in the afternoon.

'She looked very happy.'

Robert did not speak, but I could see that he was quietly delighted.

After a pause, he said:

'I was going to tell you – I suppose you must have deduced it, as Wladislaw's gone – that today I begin to pay the rent of the flat.'

'Yes,' I said: 'How does it feel?'

'It feels,' said Robert, 'like taking on a responsibility that ought to be reserved for very rich men only.'

'But you are very rich,' I said.

Robert drank a little sherry.

'Keeping two establishments going is very expensive indeed,' he said.

'Happily I don't have to worry about that,' I said, thinking of Myrtle's income. And then I recalled, unhappily, that Myrtle aimed, when we were married, at our keeping only one establishment. I drank a little of my sherry.

We paused. The old man was dozing very erratically.

'Is he here every Saturday night?' I whispered.

'He comes up to London every weekend.'

'Does his wife let him, or is she too old to care?'

'They're never too old to care, never...' Robert paused. 'He's a widower.'

In the dim light the sherry looked a deep golden colour. I said:

'I suppose it would cost less if you moved into Julia's flat.'

Robert hesitated. 'I don't think I could do that.'

I said: 'If you're dining with her tonight, it will seem an awful bore to go home afterwards.'

Robert said: 'Do you know, I've never stayed the whole night with her? Even if it's been 5 am, I've still gone home.'

I was not surprised, because I always did the same thing myself. 'If you stay till the morning, you're trapped,' I said.

Robert was silent. We became serious.

I said: 'I thought Julia was very much less racketty and tense.' I glanced at him slowly. 'You have a wonderfully good effect on her.'

'Yes,' Robert said. 'But am I to devote myself to having a good effect on her?' He looked at me. 'The poor dear needs me. And I think – I *think* if I were certain I could save her from her fate, I might take it on . .' He paused. 'I don't know. I wish to God I did. What do you think?'

I was silent. It was the first time recently that Robert had spoken so directly, and I recognised with pain a note that had run through his disastrous love affair with The Headlamps – the desire to save someone from her fate.

'I don't know,' I said, because he knew that at the bottom of my heart I did not believe in such miracles.

'I don't know if I ought to marry her,' Robert said. 'It would mean being prepared to devote myself to her pretty completely.'

I thought he was exaggerating – he had a romantic temperament.

'And,' he went on, 'there are so many other things I want to do.' His voice livened. 'We must throw off these jobs we have, and get down to what we really want to do. It's intolerable!'

'I agree.' I said gently: 'If I thought it was going to occupy you completely, looking after her, I should have to say I didn't think you ought to take it on.'

We finished our glasses of sherry. The old man had stopped breathing heavily through his whiskers and the room was silent. Robert looked thoughtful; his eyes were sparkling oddly in his impassive face, and he appeared to be speaking to himself rather than to me.

'If I did marry her, it would mean I should never know when I was going to come home and find her drunk or in bed with another man.'

I thought: 'He isn't going to marry her.'

PART IV

CHAPTER I

THE RIVALS

Myrtle unexpectedly rang me up and asked me if I would see Haxby.

I said No.

Myrtle then demanded that I should see Haxby.

I had always suspected her of wanting to arrange a scene between her two men – what woman can resist it? – but by pretending to be so stupid as not to catch on to her hints I had managed to evade it up to now. Frankly, I did not want to meet Haxby. I had nothing to say to him, and I could not help seeing that he probably did have something to say to me.

'Darling, you've got to see him. It's important.'

At that I should have had to pretend to be so stupid as not to catch on to the English language.

'What does he want?' I asked, thinking the matter might possibly be settled on the telephone.

'He'll tell you when he sees you,' said Myrtle, determined that it might not.

I gave in, and we began to arrange a rendezvous.

'I suppose it had better be on neutral territory,' I said.

'What for?' said Myrtle: 'I thought you'd want him to come round to your office.'

'Will he come?'

'If I tell him to.' Having sounded unseemlily brisk her tone suddenly dropped into melancholy. 'I don't see that it matters where you meet...'

We fixed on my office at ten o'clock the following morning.

While waiting for Haxby to come I went into Robert's office. I had the unpleasant sensation I used to experience before taking an examination.

'You ought to have seen him before,' Robert said, with muffled certainty.

It was the first I had heard about it. Robert was looking at me with distaste, as if he thought me deficient in common respect for the feelings of my fellow human-beings.

'I don't like scenes,' I said.

Robert shrugged his shoulders. 'To most people they seem essential.'

I did not reply. I particularly disliked scenes in which I started at a moral disadvantage. One of the reasons why most people welcomed scenes was because they were always so convinced of their own moral rectitude.

It was ten o'clock and there was no sign of Haxby. I had no doubt that he would come. Fate never allowed me to escape so easily. I sat glum and silent on Robert's table. I wondered if Haxby would burst into tears, or, worse still, pull out a revolver. I felt angry with Myrtle for letting me in for a scene with him, and with Haxby for not turning up punctually for it.

I went to my own office to see if he was there, and then returned. It was getting on for a quarter past ten.

I said fretfully: 'What can he possibly want to say to me that Myrtle couldn't?'

There was a pause. 'He may want to tell you,' said Robert, 'that he's going to sue you for damages. He'd get them.'

I was astonished. It was something I had never thought of. For a moment I completely forgot my approaching encounter. It was obvious from Robert's expression that he had thought of it all along. I was as staggered by the extent of my own stupidity as dazed by the prospect of having to find some thousands of pounds ready money.

'You don't mean it,' I said feebly.

At that moment there was a tap on the door and a messenger came in.

'I beg your pardon, sir, but you do know there's a gentleman waiting to see you? In the waiting room?'

'Didn't he tell you he'd got an appointment at ten?' I could scarcely believe it.

'He never told me, sir. Never said a word.'

I stamped into my office and sat down at my desk. Haxby

was shown in. Did we shake hands or not? I made a sweeping gesture with my right arm. 'Will you sit down?'

Haxby sat down.

'I was here all the time,' I said, excusing myself with some irritation. I sat down opposite him.

'I thought you must be busy,' he replied in a manner that was, I suppose, polite. He had a slight Midland accent.

'I was waiting for you,' I said.

We sat and looked at each other. In the days before the war, when Myrtle first knew him, I had slightingly described him as tall, dark and skinny. He was still tall and dark, but in the course of Army life he had clearly 'filled-out'. He was a good deal bigger and stronger than me. As for the over-intense light in his eyes, black eyes, that had been a further subject for my jealous strictures, I could only think now that I had never looked at him properly. His eyes were not even black, they were brown; and at the present moment the light in them was no more intense than his wretched circumstances warranted. His face looked haggard but it was not unpresentable. In fact, if he had not been Myrtle's husband, who was probably just about to break the news that he wanted five thousand pounds in damages, I should have thought he looked a decent, intelligent fellow.

He was wearing an Army great-coat converted to civilian style.

'Are you warm enough?' I said.

'Thanks.' He began to take off the coat.

My unpleasant pre-examination feeling seemed to have disappeared.

'It's good of you to see me,' he said.

I did not reply. There was a note of respect in his voice. I suppose I must have looked like a successful civil servant to him. I felt like saying 'Oh dear!' I was no longer irritated with him.

'We've got to talk about Myrtle,' he said, with a show of spirit.

'Yes.'

'We can't go on like this.'

'No.' I looked at him. 'Are you going to divorce her?'

'I haven't made up my mind.'

'I wish you would.'

'I'm sure you do.' Apparently he was not as supine or respectful as I had imagined.

My telephone began to ring. I did not answer it. When it stopped he said:

'I don't propose to tell you what I think about your conduct.'

I received this information with relief.

He then embarked on a somewhat protracted tirade. There was nothing original about it, but then there was nothing very original in our situation – didn't it even come into the Bible somewhere? I had tried to evade having to hear it: the longer it went on the more right I knew I had been. My moral disadvantage was total. It is all very well to feel ashamed of oneself in one's own terms, at one's own choice. In Haxby's terms and at Haxby's choice it was an odious experience.

'I don't see the point of all this,' I said. 'What's it leading up to?'

Haxby stopped. There was a moment's silence.

'You and Myrtle seemed to have worked it all out between you,' he said. 'But I'm not going to give in without a struggle.' His tone was serious and suddenly devoid of rancour. 'If Myrtle leaves me,' he said, 'I shall resign my job.'

It was the last thing I had expected. I was greatly alarmed. It seemed incredible that he should have thought of it, but that was no consolation. If he resigned his job we were back, assuming that Myrtle had not changed her mind, where we started. I saw now why she had sent him to tell me himself.

'How could you possibly live?' I asked.

Haxby did not answer me. He looked at me directly, with a steady gaze – it was intense.

'What does Myrtle say about it?' I asked.

'Nothing.'

'Wasn't it rather a stroke of luck to get the job?'

'That means nothing to me.' His gaze dropped, and we were both silent. I stared at him. I seemed to hear Myrtle's voice echoing 'He says he can't live without me.' If he had told me he was going to sue me for damages and live on the proceeds, it would have been a situation with a definite outcome. But proving that he could not live without her by being permanently out of work – I saw no end to that.

'I know she's always been in love with you,' he said. He paused. 'I've always been in love with her.'

And he looked up. His eyes were bright black with emotion. 'Oh God.'

The telephone rang again. I did not answer it.

'Are you determined to make three people unhappy?' I said. 'Have you thought of that?'

'I have.'

'You've admitted that Myrtle's in love with me.'

'*That doesn't mean she'd be unhappy if she went on being married to me.*'

I stopped in a burst of surprise. He did not repeat his remark, yet I felt as though he did. I felt as if I had suddenly heard a prophetic revelation, that expressed the truth for all of us.

The telephone rang again – I could not think why on earth my p.a. was letting the calls get through.

I stood up.

At that, Haxby stood up. He glanced finally round the office.

'Busy, aren't you?' he said.

CHAPTER II

AN IMPARTIAL REPORT

Dr Chubb returned from his second tour exhausted, but apparently satisfied. What he had said and done this time, we did not know. Robert refused to confront him with the rumours about his first tour because they were so contradictory: I suspected Robert of letting Chubb have his head to make a serious blunder.

Nothing happened. A week passed and there were no reports from our personal friends in the firms on Chubb's itinerary. Perhaps Chubb had heard the rumours himself: perhaps none of them had been true. Perhaps – I have to admit that the possibility did occur to us – Chubb had become a loyal and discreet member of D.O.R.R.S.

The information had been collected. With nothing else to distract us for the time being, we were able to concentrate on preparing a report. Sir Francis decided to write the report himself, and no tactful offers of assistance could head him off. We were alarmed because he had to present the report to an inter-departmental committee at their next meeting. At the end of a week he was three days behind schedule.

'Why can't he let me write it?' said Robert.

By staying up all through one night, Sir Francis completed his task. The draft appeared on Robert's desk, and he spent a couple of hours reading it. Nobody could deny that Sir Francis had presented all the facts. It must have been one of the most comprehensive reports ever written. The order was logical, the structure was perfect. Sir Francis had displayed the grasp that was appropriate to his inordinately high degree of intelligence. The only trouble with his report was that it was impossible to gather the gist of it.

You will recall that the function of D.O.R.R.S. was to present facts impartially. No man could have been more devastatingly equipped by temperament to carry it out – Sir Francis could judge impartiality to perfection: he could raise it to the level of sheer meaninglessness.

'I think we may reasonably expect the committee to say,' he announced proudly, 'that we have not been guilty of giving them a lead of any description!'

Robert rang for me to come to his office and read the document as soon as he had finished with it. I gave up at the fifth page.

Robert was standing abstractedly by the window, watching the traffic in Parliament Square.

'The report ought not to have been more than three pages long,' he said. 'And then an enormous twenty-page appendix with all his figures in it.'

'Why don't you write one yourself and then persuade him to scrap this?'

Robert shook his head. 'He'd never agree.' He turned to me. 'How could he possibly see what was wrong with his own?'

Up to this moment we had been looking forward to the resolution of the controversy with growing excitement. We were far from impartial ourselves, and we expected the satisfaction of seeing our side win.

We had put our money – in the purely metaphorical sense, I am bound to point out in view of what certain other persons did – on the A 16. No doubt it looks easy for me to be right after the event, but it seems to me still that Robert's way of arriving at a conclusion was the most sensible. Anybody could see that the A 16, as it then stood, was not a workable proposition: the question was whether it could ever be made one, and if so, by whom.

It was our conviction that in all scientific discoveries and inventions, a major creative active act, on the part of one man only, happened in the first place. It was difficult to predict when such a man would turn up: he was born, not made, and in the world's history did not seem to be born very often. But once a major step forward had been taken, the rest could perfectly well be carried out by men of moderate originality, provided they were equipped with the necessary technique – the thing for which modern civilisation really had fitted itself was the production of such persons in fair quantity.

As far as the A 16 was concerned, the major creative act had been performed, the revolutionary step was manifest. Somehow or other, instinct told us, the rest of the work would get done. Time, money and men – we could scarcely believe the Americans were not already ahead of us. Had Dr Chubb been let loose in America they probably would have been.

Such considerations had no appeal whatsoever to the mind of Sir Francis. 'Somehow or other' was neither just nor accurate, so it was meaningless to him. 'We must look into it much more deeply than that, my dear Robert,' he said, with his head sagaciously cocked on one side. More questionnaires to industrial firms, more contingency tables, more reports.

On the other hand I must not give the impression that Sir Francis was impartial in his own personal opinions. He was quite certain that his report, properly construed – and it never occurred to him that other people would have the greatest difficulty in construing it at all – proved that we ought to go ahead with the A 16 without delay, and indicated to the department which firms should be given development contracts. 'It's all there,' he said, with triumphant cunning. It was. Among us all, the only person who obtusely insisted that the case was not proven was James.

Suddenly Robert came across to his desk and took the draft from me.

'I don't see why I shouldn't tell him what I think,' he said. 'I'm not going to be here for ever.' He took out his fountain-pen. He framed his comment, and then handed it to me to read with a subdued grin. It was formally addressed to D.O.R.R.S.

I am afraid this makes it very difficult to see the wood for the trees.

Signed with Robert's initials and dated.

I rang for his personal assistant to take the document away.

When she had gone his grin disappeared. He shook his head.

'If Old Frank doesn't see sense in time, he'll really get into hot water over this.'

CHAPTER III

SOMEONE NEW ON THE SCENE

The following day we went to a cocktail party at Sir Francis's house. During the afternoon the snow came back again. People watched the falling curtain of flakes with claustrophobic annoyance. It was intolerable.

The party was on the occasion of Sir Francis's only son Jocelyn's return from military service in the Far East, and Robert and I were invited to bring our young women. Sir Francis was aware that our private lives were what he was accustomed to consider bohemian, in fact we knew that was why he so enthusiastically asked us to bring Julia and Myrtle. No detail eluded Sir Francis in his energetic pursuit of fair-mindedness: he regarded our bohemianism as a satisfactory corrective to his own stiffly conventional behaviour.

The invitations had been given several weeks earlier, and Myrtle had promised to come up to London specially for the party. Consequently our meeting for the first time since my scene with Haxby was to come about automatically. I waited for her to pick me up after the office feeling distinctly apprehensive. It was clear that Robert, waiting for Julia, was feeling apprehensive too: I strongly suspected that he and Julia had been quarrelling recently. We stood at the window, watching Parliament Square under a leaden sky gradually lose its sharp outlines in a veil of thin greyish snow. Lights flashed miserably from windows and moving headlamps.

Quite apart from our general apprehensions about the future of our disordered lives, Robert and I were feeling a specific apprehension about what was likely to happen in the next few hours, when it seemed quite likely, in view of the circumstances, that our girls would get drunk.

'Damn the snow,' I said.

Robert ignored me. He was holding a handkerchief to his nose: he had a cold.

Myrtle and Julia came in together. They were chattering gaily, and expressed their surprise at finding us not radiant with pleasurable excitement. They were obviously out for alcohol, and looked as if they had had some already. I wondered what Julia had been saying to Myrtle – advising her not to sit down under something or other, I presumed.

We hired a taxi to Sir Francis's house, which was in Chester Street. The party was held on the first floor, in a handsome parqueted salon made by knocking two rooms together. At the end of the smaller part, beside a service hatch in which a little lift kept rumbling up and down, there was a bar-table set up by a professional firm of caterers. Sir Francis was a widower and had no women-folk to entertain for him. There were two fires glowing brilliantly in marble fireplaces, and the light sparkled from two small chandeliers.

Sir Francis received us formally and introduced Jocelyn, an elegant handsome youth in the Brigade of Guards. Sir Francis was a devoted father and his bright intelligent eyes were shining, his antennae-like eyebrows almost sparking with innocent pleasure in showing off his son – and, it has to be admitted, with innocent hope that one of the guests might offer the boy a job when he resigned his commission.

People were arriving in crowds, so we went immediately to the bar. I held Myrtle's hand to prevent us from getting separated, and then led her to the opposite end of the room. There were two long windows overlooking Chester Street, and the opulent dark blue curtains had been left undrawn – the white-painted lines of the window frames gleamed in rectangles across the darkness outside. We stood by a small mahogany table on which there was a vase containing leafless sprays, over three feet long, of beautiful, heavy, mauve lilac.

Myrtle unconcernedly sipped her drink and then sniffed the flowers. 'They don't smell.'

'They're hot-house. They never do.'

'They look lovely, all the same,' she murmured. I noticed with surprise that she was wearing a hat.

'Do you like it?' she asked.

While I was trying to find an answer, she ran her finger over the surface of the table. She said:

'He has some lovely furniture. I bet this is Sheraton.'

'He's quite a wealthy man.'

'Then why is he a civil servant?'

We stared at each other. I ignored the question. I could bear idle conversation no longer.

'What did Dennis say after I'd seen him?'

Myrtle's eyes looked round and light brown and innocent. 'Nothing that he hadn't said before, darling.'

'What's he going to do?'

'Give up his job if I leave him.'

'Then what are you going to do?'

'What am I going to do, darling? I honestly don't know. I can't think any more.' She looked at me. 'I wish you would tell me.'

'I?' I cried. 'I've done nothing but tell you. Leave him! Marry me!'

Myrtle shook her head sadly. 'That's too easy, darling.'

'Why should its being easy be a reason for not doing it? Do you prefer to do something difficult?'

Myrtle did not smile. 'Suppose I did leave him, what would he do?' she said, looking into her glass.

'He'd find himself another woman,' I said promptly. 'That sort of man always does.'

Myrtle glanced at me with naif interest. 'Would you, if I didn't marry you?'

'No.'

Myrtle was thoughtful. Having come out with the truth, I also was thoughtful – well I might be, as I had given two wrong answers in succession.

Before I could think of a remedy, our conversation was interrupted by James Irskine and his wife. James took me aside while the women were speaking to each other. 'I saw Robert's minute to Old Frank,' he said: 'I couldn't agree more.'

'What did the old boy say?'

'He took it rather well.'

James glared at me, and I did my best to glare back. Then we both turned to look in Sir Francis's direction. Sir Francis was talking animatedly to Robert, and at that moment Robert broke into laughter.

I wondered where Julia was, and found her in a little group surrounding Jocelyn Plumer. I went across to her, and took her away from them. She had been drinking rapidly. Her eyes were bright and bulging and furtive, and the skin at the base of her throat was reddening.

'Tell me who all these people are?' she said, to forestall any serious remark from me. 'I mean the men, of course.'

I pointed out numerous distinguished civil servants, a junior minister, one or two people who were plainly aristocratic, and one or two industrial figures who included Lord —— . I thought they looked very much like successful men from any walk of life. They were mostly heavy, vigorous creatures, with bodies that must have been meaty and powerful. At first sight some of them looked not particularly clever – what characterised all their faces was a permeating confidence and will. I was interested to observe what a high proportion of them had plain wives. I did not really find it an attractive gathering of people. I explained to Julia our function in counter-balancing their respectability. She was delighted with the idea.

'Dear Old Frank,' I said. 'He must think *we* carry an awful lot of guns.'

'*Their* armament may not be as heavy as it looks,' said Julia, and laughed somewhat intoxicatedly at her own joke. Suddenly she leaned towards me.

'I'll tell you who's on our side,' she said, and fixed me with a knowing stare. 'Jocelyn.'

'Is he?' I had paid no attention to him. Suddenly I realised that Julia was no longer looking at me, but was looking back through the crowd at him.

I waited for her attention to return. She said: 'I want another drink.' A waiter was passing with a tray. She said to me: 'I suppose you know Robert and I have had another row.'

'I guessed as much. What about?'

'I'm not going to tell you.' Suddenly she burst out. 'I'm

getting very impatient.'

'That won't do you any good with Robert.'

'I can't help it!' She now looked across at Robert, and the grip on her glass tightened. Then it relaxed.

Robert was talking weightily to Lord ——. He was holding his handkerchief.

Julia said: 'He doesn't want to take me home. He says he's got a cold.' Her high spirits seemed to have gone and her tone had a sharp disharmonious edge. 'I shall stay here and drink.' She paused. 'I suppose you're taking Myrtle back?'

'I hope so.'

'If I were you, I should be impatient with her.'

'I am.'

I was sure Julia must be recalling a conversation they had held earlier in the evening. She said:

'I think we both ought to cut our losses.'

'What does that mean? And who's we?'

'Myrtle and me.'

'What do you mean about Myrtle?'

Julia said:

'I don't think Myrtle ought to marry you.'

I was angry. 'Why not?' I cried.

'I don't think she'd settle down with you.' Julia's voice was still harsh. 'I don't think she's made for you. If you want to know why – to put it simply, I think she needs a husband where she can wear the trousers.'

At first I was too angry to reply. It was the explanation of all average people, all *hommes moyens sensuels* and their female equivalents.

'I hope you didn't tell her that!'

Julia did not reply. Of course she had told her – and a great deal more besides, I did not doubt.

Julia gave a forced laugh. She said: 'In any case, she ought to leave her husband.'

At this I really was dumbfounded. There was a long pause. I stared at Julia. I thought she had a slightly crazed look or else she was drunk. I said:

'Are you trying to break up everything? And if so, in heaven's name, why?'

She stared back at me.

'You don't understand.' She spoke penetratingly. 'You don't understand that I'm feeling antagonistic. Towards everyone.'

I thought she really was slightly mad. She took hold of my wrist and did not speak again for a few moments. I felt sorry for her, even if she had been treacherously exhorting Myrtle not to sit down under my presumed dominance.

'Poor old Julia! . . .'

Julia said: 'If you only knew the difficulty I'm having, in not throwing this drink in your face!'

I thought it was time for me to move along to one of the other guests. I looked back and saw Julia moving towards Jocelyn Plumer.

'Joe!' It was Robert. 'I'm going home now.' While he spoke to me his eyes were fixed on Julia. 'My cold's getting worse.'

'Julia thinks Old Frank's son is not specially respectable. She says he's on our side.' I felt as if I were somehow trying to explain away Julia's conduct.

Robert said nothing while we watched her. Before I had time to say anything else, he went away. I looked at my watch. It was time I too left the party. Myrtle was not going to stay the night in London. I went to find her.

As Myrtle and I said goodbye to Sir Francis, I glanced over his shoulder. I saw Julia talking to Jocelyn: she was standing very close to him. At that moment she glanced towards us. She waved with great zest.

CHAPTER IV

ANOTHER FOND FAREWELL

From the time when we left the party Myrtle and I got on steadily better together. The snow was falling lightly and we got a taxi straight away. When Myrtle heard me give the driver the address of my house she demurred.

'Hadn't we better go straight to Euston?' she said.

'No, darling,' said I.

'But, darling . . .'

'Yes?'

She gave me a soulful look.

'Didn't you expect we should be going back to the flat first?' I said.

Myrtle shook her head, looked through the window of the taxi, and then looked reproachfully at me.

'You didn't warn me, darling,' she said with plaintive emphasis.

'Oh come! . . .'

Myrtle pretended to make a short hopeless search through the contents of her handbag.

I looked at her with astonishment, hardly able to believe her, Myrtle, a married woman of long standing. She shook her head again, to indicate that making love was unfortunately impossible. Immediately I was taken back to the days of our first affair: whenever there was anything wrong this was exactly the trick she had played on me – I could never believe it was not a trick.

And being taken back eight years, my response to the trick was exactly the same – extraordinary determination not to submit to it. What had seemed to me a purely enjoyable experience a few minutes ago, was now transformed into a passionate necessity. I made this clear to Myrtle. She looked as if she was quite unable to understand me. Age had not altered us a scrap: the years had taught us absolutely nothing. The taxi skidded round by Victoria station.

'I know where there's a little shop that will still be open,' I said.

'How do you know?' said Myrtle, suspiciously.

'I've used it before.'

She was furiously jealous. I shouted instructions to the driver, and sat back in the corner opposite to her. I thought she had got what she asked for.

You may think all this was no improvement in our relations, but somehow it was. We were back in a familiar domestic wrangle whose outcome was always harmonious, and we both knew it – you see, I still think Myrtle had done it on purpose.

We went rapidly upstairs to my flat. I put a match to the gas-fire in the bedroom and it gave a feeble glow. I put a shilling in the meter, and was rewarded by a glow that was feebler if anything. Outside it was snowing: I expected Myrtle to say she was cold enough to die. Instead she said with melancholy interest: 'What have you done with the whisky, darling?'

On my knees by the hearth, I looked up at her.

'A gas-fire doesn't really warm a girl's heart,' she said.

When I was on my feet again I embraced her. I had forgotten that until she married me I was supposed to give an air of passive suffering. I thought 'Dammit, I'm going to be myself!' I was filled with a delightful inflatory mixture of optimism and triumph. I felt that Myrtle might as well get used to me as I was, because that was how I was going to be after we were married. It seemed to me that this was an evening I had been waiting for. I had put up with doubts and hesitations long enough. Tonight was going to settle it: all was going to be well.

I put my watch where it was easily visible, so that we should not miss the time for Myrtle's last train.

'What are you doing that for, darling?' she said.

I explained.

Myrtle sighed and put her arms round my neck. I recalled

her provocative trick that had failed. Mixed optimism and triumph inflated me still further.

By the time we were ready to leave the flat, Myrtle seemed to be inflated too. Her eyes were luminous and the corners of her mouth twitched as if she were amused without knowing it. I humoured her with another nip of whisky and hurried her downstairs. While I was telephoning in the hall for a taxi, Mrs Burdup came past and Myrtle deliberately made her stop and discuss the weather.

It was snowing fast now. In the slit of light from the doorway behind us we saw flakes floating down, silently, mysteriously. The taxi came up and we jumped in.

It was a romantic ride. The road was thickly covered, and the glow round each street-lamp was so reduced that we seemed to be travelling from one little world of drifting spots of light to another. I put my arms round Myrtle and held her close to me. She was warm and sweet-smelling. I kissed her. Her coat fell open. I drew her much closer. She lifted her head quickly.

'Oh, darling! . . .'

'What?' We were whispering to each other.

'What about the driver?'

'Taxi-drivers are used to it! . . .'

Over her shoulder I saw the dark shadow of the driver's back, motionless. He was wearing a cap. I felt Myrtle's body relax a little. I drew her over, and she sighed loudly in my ear. The taxi went on through the night, inexorably.

Suddenly, under a street-lamp, the taxi stopped. With a muffled cry Myrtle jumped off my lap, and hit her head on the roof. We saw the driver get out. Myrtle flung herself into the corner of the cab. He began to wipe snow off the windscreen – the wiper had jammed. We laughed with relief.

Sitting in opposite corners Myrtle and I could see each other dimly. We did not say anything, but she stretched out her hand to me and I held it. We felt far away from everything in the gentle silence and darkness of the night. The snow was all round us. The driver was whistling quietly to himself – we were not lonely. Our hearts, our souls were expanding. It was like being in youthful love again, warm, tender, ineffable.

With a faint click and a whirr the wiper began to work again. The driver got back into his seat and we drove off. We were somewhere in Bloomsbury. I looked at my watch.

'What was Robert saying to you just before we left the party?'

It was the first time in the evening that Myrtle had shown any concern for my affairs. She spoke in a light conversational tone.

It seemed no time at all before we were at Euston. We were friends as well as lovers.

I gave the driver a large tip.

Myrtle was watching me, with a slyly innocent expression that could not have been more explicit if she had actually been saying 'conscience-money'.

'Come along,' I said, haughtily. The station seemed unusually deserted, though there was no reason why a snowstorm in London should discourage people from travelling to Birmingham or Glasgow. Myrtle linked her arm through mine.

We chose a compartment, and the time came for us to make our last speeches. My optimism and triumph had given place to a stable confidence and happiness. I was certain that tonight she must make up her mind to leave Haxby. I felt I must say something to mark the occasion, rather as a good civil servant feels the compulsion to put something down on paper. I looked into Myrtle's face, trying to frame all that was in my heart. I did not know how to put it.

We went out on to the platform, and I slipped my arm round Myrtle's waist. 'It's been wonderful,' I muttered.

Myrtle gave me a long tremulous look. And then she said:

'Don't worry, darling. It will come out to *us* in the end.'

Whether anybody was watching us or not, I clasped her tightly in my arms. I was thinking 'I'll love you and keep you for ever.'

CHAPTER V

SIR FRANCIS ACTS

Next morning, in spite of his cold, Robert came bustling into the office early.

'Old Frank's sent for me.'

There was no time for our usual conversation. Robert was smiling with amusement: he was certain that Sir Francis was going to ask him to re-write the report.

While Robert was in conference with Sir Francis, I cheerfully picked up the draft and began to work out my own ideas of what it should be.

Robert returned with a very unusual expression.

'Isn't he going to let you do it after all?' I asked.

'Oh yes, that's all right.' He sat down close to me on the corner of my desk. 'As a matter of fact, there's something else afoot.' He paused, glanced away and then back again. 'Old Frank has just heard that Lord ——'s firm is already well ahead with something on the lines of the A 16.'

I exclaimed.

Robert stared at me, with his eyes looking bright and sharp.

'It's pretty surprising, I agree.'

Lord —— was chairman of the biggest group of industries in the federation of which he was president. He was neither a fool nor a gambler.

'Old Frank is astounded,' Robert went on. 'He thinks there must have been a breach of security somewhere.'

'Security!'

'You forget how seriously he takes all our formal precautions. He still imagines the firms don't know exactly why we've been making our survey. As for the side we're going to come down on – he doesn't believe yet that we really have come down. Let alone that Lord —— could have guessed it.'

'Guessed it?' I said. 'Guessed it, my foot!' I stared at Robert. 'Lord —— has heard something, and I bet you we know where.'

Robert's face became more impassive and his eyes sparkled more brightly. There was a pause.

'What's Old Frank going to do?' I said. 'Ring up Lord —— and congratulate him on his good sense?'

'You ought to know better than that. Nothing of the kind. Far, far from it. He's asked Lord —— to meet him, to confront him with a supposed breach of security and to ask him to explain it.'

CHAPTER VI

SELF-SACRIFICING FRIENDSHIP

L ater that morning I got a message asking me to telephone
Mr Łempicki-Czyz immediately.

I rang Wladislaw at his office in the City. He wanted me to
meet him as soon as possible.

'What's the matter?' I asked.

'It is not possible to tell you on the telephone.' His strong
nasal voice made the diaphragm rattle. 'The exchange-girl
listens.'

I always assumed our operator had too much to do: she
must have heard some surprising things if she had not. I
agreed to meet Wladislaw in the Berkeley Hotel at six o'clock.

I was a little late, but Wladislaw had not arrived. The
irregular-shaped room with mirrors where one had drinks was
almost empty, so I chose a corner table suited to a *tête-à-tête*.
Wladislaw came in. He was dressed for business, in an
excellently cut black pin-stripe suit and a white shirt. His tie
was made of glistening sombre silk, with a pearl tie-pin
planted in the middle of it. Somehow, one would have known
at sight that he was a foreigner – not by his clothes, but by the
shape of him: I thought he was too cubical to be English. He
sat down and called for a waiter.

It was impossible to tell what was the matter. Wladislaw's
massive powerful face was not made for expressing emotion,
and I imagined the only thing that could alter his piercing look
was a mixture of rage and sexual desire – which no doubt made
it more piercing.

Wladislaw ordered two whiskies and soda, and after we had
taken the ritual first sip, he said, with his head bent:

'I have some unfortunate news.' He glanced at me. 'About

Julia.'

'I saw her last night, at a party given by my boss.'

'Yes.' Wladislaw looked at me fixedly. 'I know. She met there a young man named Jocelyn Plumer' – he pronounced the J in a continental fashion – 'and after the party she took him home with her. For the night. She was drunk.' Wladislaw watched for my response.

I was not so much surprised by the information as puzzled by how he knew.

I said: 'Did she tell you?'

'No,' said Wladislaw. 'I have her watched. By private detective.' He delivered the explanation with straightforward moral rectitude.

'Really!' I have to confess that I was shocked. Had my self-restraint been only a shade weaker I could have told Waldislaw it was not playing the game. I said: 'You don't mean to say you employ someone to spy on her?'

'Why not?'

'If you don't see it for yourself, I really doubt if I can explain it you.'

'I want to know what she is doing,' Wladislaw said. 'I have her watched all the time.'

'But the money it must cost you!' I said, momentarily forgetting about playing the game.

'It is necessary.'

'That's a matter for argument.'

'Not at all. It's necessary for me to know what she's doing. It's necessary for me to have her watched, constantly.'

I said slyly: 'For your own ends . . .'

'No.' Wladislaw now spoke to me with great, direct force. '*It is for her good!*'

I had no reply to make to that.

Wladislaw's small bright grey eyes seemed to glance piercingly through to the back of my skull. His voice was lower. 'Everything I do is for her good. When I offer her my friendship, it is for her good. When I sacrifice my own deeper feelings, it is for her good.'

There was a long pause. 'Then that's all there is to be said.' I drank a little whisky. If only, I thought, Wladislaw had the faintest sense of humour, I might have made some impression on him. So incapable was he of looking into his own self-seeking motives, so entirely lacking in any kind of detachment when judging himself, that he genuinely did believe every word he was saying.

'I am willing to do anything to make Julia happy,' he said. 'And I am convinced she cannot be happy leading this sort of life. She has fallen back into her old ways. We must save her.'

I could not resist pretending not to cotton on. I said hollowly: 'I doubt if there's much we can do.'

'There is always much we can do.'

I shook my head. 'One can't really save anybody.' I looked at him. 'People can't really be seriously changed.'

'If you think people can't really be changed,' Wladislaw said quickly, with his eyes flashing, 'then it follows that they cannot be saved! I think people can be saved... That is because I believe people can be changed! I disagree with your premise. When you say Julia cannot be saved, it is because your premise is false. How' – he wound up with incisiveness that would not have done discredit to Sir Francis – 'can you expect to reach correct conclusions from false premises?'

I felt as if the breath had been knocked out of me. Second only to his passion for Julia was Wladislaw's passion for abstract argument. And abstract argument of this kind was entirely outside my range. How could I expect to reach correct conclusions from false premises? I had no idea.

Wladislaw was still giving me a formidably flashing stare. He awaited a logical reply.

'I doubt if we can alter Julia very much,' I said doggedly.

Wladislaw must have been feeling a mixture of disappointment and plain contempt. He sat back in his chair and drank some more whisky. He clearly did not think I was very clever. He said:

'I think we can save her from these self-destructive acts.'

Neither of us had the wit to remember that Julia got a good deal of enjoyment out of what we portentously called her self-destructive acts.

I said: 'I doubt if this was as serious as all that. She was piqued because Robert wouldn't take her home, so she took someone else.' I warmed up to my thesis. 'A lot of Julia's acts are devised for their effect on a third person.'

'I am sorry the acts are all of the same kind!'

I could not escape the feeling that I had lost another argument.

Wladislaw put down his glass and felt to see if his pearl tie-pin was in place.

'I want to know if you are willing to help me, to try to save her.'

It crossed my mind that he was a madman.

'How?'

'I want your advice about it.'

'Yes?'

'Do you think,' said Wladislaw uncunningly, 'you should tell Robert immediately?'

'Why? Do you want him to quarrel with her?'

Wladislaw paused. I wondered – did a flicker of comprehension suddenly illuminate him?

'He has great influence on Julia.' He began weightily to develop the idea.

I tried to head him off by saying: 'She'll probably tell Robert herself.'

There was a short pause.

'Then do you think,' said Wladislaw, with apparent diffidence, 'you should tell Jocelyn Plumer about me?'

I was unable to conceal my astonishment and respect. This really was a cunning manoeuvre. It took a very strong-minded youth not to be put off when he heard his mistress was being shadowed by another lover's detective, that lover being a rich Polish businessman.

'I don't know him,' I said.

Wladislaw said methodically: 'Robert knows him.'

'Well, really!' I banged my glass down on the table.

Wladislaw turned to look at me. I judged him to be surprised.

'Do you not wish to help me?' he asked. And there was strong appealing emotion in his voice.

The only thing to do was to answer in his own terms. 'I should like to,' I said, with equal fervour. I had got my next remark ready.

'Then perhaps you will speak to Robert tomorrow.'

'I will if I decide it's compatible with my friendship for Julia.'

Wladislaw understood that.

I had not the slightest intention of telling anybody anything. There was a long silence.

'I do everything for Julia's own good. I want no reward.' Wladislaw looked at me for a long time. 'Like you, I do only what is compatible with friendship.'

I did not know whether to laugh, shout at him with rage, or just stay silent. I stayed silent. There he sat, with his neck as wide as his face and his narrow eyes alight with power and sincerity. Of course he was not mad. He was only different from me.

CHAPTER VII

'WILL IT END PUNCTUALLY?'

Sir Francis had arranged his meeting for a quarter past four on the following day. He told us that he had impressed Lord —— with the importance of the occasion. At this Robert shook his head gloomily. It happened that Chubb had taken two days' leave: he was summoned to return. That cheered us up.

When Robert and I arrived at Sir Francis's room, he was busy in his personal assistant's office, so we had the place to ourselves. On the polished mahogany table there was a tray holding white earthenware cups and saucers. While we stood looking through the window a messenger brought in a plate of fancy cakes which Sir Francis had punctiliously sent him out to buy at an A.B.C.

In Parliament Square the snow was melting for the second time, and we could not help feeling a quite disproportionate relief.

'It gives one some idea of how people in the Middle Ages must have felt at the first signs of spring,' said Robert, in a tone which indicated that his imagination was ranging far beyond the scope of mine.

The messenger came in again carrying a big brown enamel tea-pot. I meditated on spring and summer – something made me recall the afternoon when Robert and I had contemplated the striped awning outside St Margaret's. I meditated on summer and divorce and fate.

Chubb came in. I thought he looked more hare-eyed than usual, and also ruddier of cheek.

'I hope this meeting is going to end punctually,' he said, giving Robert a toothy, and, I thought, frightened smile. 'I mean, it was rather inconvenient for me to come to this meeting at all. I've arranged to take my wife to the theatre tonight – it isn't often she gets a chance to go, with it being so difficult about servants in these days – so I don't want to be late. As it is, she'll have to wait for me in my club. Fortunately there's a ladies' room . . .'

He was very nervous.

'I think it rather depends on Plumer,' Robert said, as if he were taking the conversation seriously.

I reflected upon the unusual frequency with which people happened to be ill or on leave at the moment when they were about to find themselves in trouble.

'I suppose we'd better wait for our tea.' Chubb stood by the table and eyed the cakes. Big Ben chimed a quarter past.

The door opened and in came Sir Francis and Lord ——, followed by James Irskine. Sir Francis looked pink and bright-eyed; his antennae-like eyebrows were curling. Lord —— glanced at the table as he came over to shake hands with Robert.

'Tea and cakes!' he said, in the booming, important voice in which one might say 'War and peace!' or 'Love and death!'

I had never been able to prevent myself from thinking Lord —— was an ass. I was quite wrong. He was a big heavy man with a very slight stoop, and he had a completely bald egg-shaped head. It always seemed to me that his voice boomed so much because it was resounding inside his egg-shaped head. He was a very clever, able man. Nobody but a clever and able man could have reached the presidency of his particular federation, where his competitors for the honour were in my opinion so clever and able that they might have been thought dishonest.

Lord —— then turned to Chubb, who returned the false affable smile fading from Lord ——'s face, with a nervous sycophantic laugh.

'I didn't reckon on our meeting again so soon,' said Chubb.

'Very interesting. Very interesting,' said Lord ——, with a particularly disinterested boom, and turned away from him.

We sat down at the table, and James poured out the tea in a grumpy efficient manner, as if he thought the messenger ought to have been called in, even though he could do it so much more competently himself. Chubb refused a cake. Robert took one and chewed it abstractedly. Lord —— chose the best.

While we made polite preliminary conversation, I recalled the first time I had seen Lord ——, sitting at the next table in a restaurant. Gifted with a voice that would have carried to the gallery of the Albert Hall, Lord —— had cultivated the knack of commanding by sideways glances the attention of everyone sitting round about him. He had a big nose, and large, round grey eyes in deep sockets. Seeing from his sideways glances that everyone was being forced to listen to him, his eyes glowed with pleasure and satisfaction. He was not unamiable. He merely liked to be addressing the whole room rather than the person he was speaking to, and had found a happy way of doing both.

Lord —— put the last piece of his cake into his mouth. Sir Francis instantly glanced at the clock and said:

'Shall we begin?'

'Any time you like,' said Lord ——, not in the least put out. I suddenly felt Sir Francis was going to get the worst of the exchange. And then I glanced at Dr Chubb. He was smiling his characteristic fixed hare-eyed smile. I could not believe he did not know what he was going to get.

CHAPTER VIII

HOW THE MEETING ENDED

'I think you know, Lord ——, why I've asked you to come here today.' Sir Francis put his head slightly on one side, and spoke in a most courteous manner. Yet to my mind there was something arrogant about the way he said 'I'. He clearly thought Lord —— was in a weak moral position.

'I thought it wisest to ask you to meet us, so that I could ask one or two questions quite directly.' Sir Francis gave him an even more courteous smile. 'And receive equally direct answers.'

Lord —— looked at him fixedly without speaking. Had Lord ——'s head really been an egg it could not have displayed more beautiful unresponsive poise. Sir Francis was not discouraged by it. He went on briskly.

'Two days ago it came to my ears that the firm of which you are chairman is engaged on work closely connected with the A 16. It would be both indiscreet and improper to disclose the source of my information – I am sure you will understand that – '

Sir Francis paused for Lord —— to assent. Lord —— gave no sign whatever.

'As a matter of fact,' Sir Francis said, foolishly, 'I gave my word that I would not disclose it.'

'You surprise me,' Lord ——'s voice boomed.

'Indeed?' said Sir Francis.

'I am always very careful about giving my word. Especially in such circumstances as those you mention.' He nodded his egg-head gravely while managing to glance at the rest of us to make sure we were impressed.

'I'm sure I was right to do so,' said Sir Francis, nettled.

'As you will.' The boom was the boom of an ass, and yet he contrived to make Sir Francis look childish. He was helped by the fact that he was big and Sir Francis small.

Sir Francis was about to speak, when Lord —— smiling now, interrupted him. 'I should say that gossip, by definition, is something a man promises to keep secret while not intending to do so.'

'I hope you'll assure me,' Sir Francis said smartly, 'that this was idle gossip and not the truth.'

Lord —— gave him a stare for his pains.

'Is it idle gossip?' Sir Francis asked.

'The organisation of which I am chairman,' said Lord ——, 'is indeed turning its energy towards the production of A 16s at a future date.' He paused. 'I can answer your question frankly.'

The two of them stared at each other.

'I am astonished, Lord ——. I cannot understand how such a thing can possibly have happened without a break in our security arrangements.' He gave Lord —— an account of the limited number of people in the government service who were supposed to know about the A 16, ending up: 'And it's quite unthinkable that such information should find its way to the general public.'

'I think the organisation of which I am chairman can hardly be referred to as the general public.' Lord —— laughed loudly.

Sir Francis replied with some heat, and Lord —— answered him back. They wrangled together. I glanced round the table. Robert was sitting in his usual abstracted gloom, Chubb was looking worried, James Irskine was looking blank.

'Look here, Sir Francis,' said Lord ——, beginning to get angry, 'it's unrealistic, and you must know it, to suppose that we leaders of industry don't know that a new —— is coming along.' Instead of saying A 16 he actually named the machine.

'I beg your pardon!' said Sir Francis. 'We have been instructed that in no circumstances are we to refer to it as anything other than A 16.'

Lord —— gave several sideways looks round the table. I caught a glimpse of his glowing, compelling, actor's eye – it was attractive and I almost returned the smirk of a confederate. K.Y.M.S. I wrote hastily on my blotting-pad.

'I fail to see,' Lord —— said, 'how I could discuss the capacity of my firm for making the A 16, how I could discuss that capacity with a member of your staff, if I didn't know what it was.' He changed his tone. 'I will be more than frank with you. I'll tell you that I discussed the A 16 quite openly with my friend Chubb, here – no, don't interrupt me – I discussed it with him quite openly, because there was nothing he had to tell me that I didn't know already.'

'Is this true, Dr Chubb?' said Sir Francis, so horrified as apparently not to hear Lord ——'s last sentence.

'Well, yes...' said Chubb.

'You must take it, Sir Francis,' said Lord ——, 'that a thing of such great importance cannot be kept as secret as you appear to imagine.'

Sir Francis could not speak for a moment.

Lord —— went on. 'You can rest assured that Dr Chubb disclosed none of your secrets to me.' Suddenly he sent a booming laugh round the table that seemed to draw us all into its ambit. 'There were one or two things about the A 16 that I told *him!*'

'I take leave to be my own judge of the activities of my staff!'

There was a sudden pause. Chubb said: 'I wonder if I might say something. It's quite true, what Lord —— says, and I'm sure I was perfectly aware of the degree of secrecy surrounding A 16 and would on no account have overstepped the bounds of secrecy. But talks could only proceed usefully if there was a bit of give-and-take on both sides.' His nervousness abated a little, as commonsense took possession of him. 'It's obvious that more people knew about the A 16 than we listed. They had to know and they were bound to find out, but it doesn't mean anyone did anything wrong. We're all in this thing together – the safety of the country depends on it, as everyone knows, who finds out the smallest thing about it. When we're all in it together, like that, I don't see why the secret isn't as safe with Lord —— and his firm's research team as it is with us.'

It is fair to say that Sir Francis did not see it in that way at all. He was about to speak when Lord —— bore him down again. I was interested that Lord —— was exerting himself so far. Then suddenly I recalled that whatever the general breakdown in our security arrangements happened to be, Lord ——'s firm, and none of the others in his federation, had gone ahead with the A 16. Sir Francis had shrewdly observed it right at the beginning. Lord —— had boomed grandiloquently but his moral position was not as strong as all that.

It was clear that Sir Francis was going to deliver himself of his second accusation quite soon.

Lord —— raised his voice still more resonantly. As his bald head moved to and fro with greater amplitude the reflected light flashed from it.

'I don't deny your right to be your own judge of the activities of your staff, Sir Francis. All of us take that right. But I feel bound to say that I, and I believe you too, have reason to congratulate Dr Chubb on the part he has played in this affair. You can be assured that he definitely behaved with complete propriety regarding the restrictions of security. At the same time I found him most helpful. I found him even' – he glanced in passing first at Robert and then at me – 'statesman-like. It was as much due to his sage counsel as to anyone's, that the organisation of which I am chairman, decided to go ahead with the A 16!'

Chubb turned pale. White patches appeared below his eyes.

It was clear that Sir Francis could scarcely believe his ears. His own sense of propriety was so strong that it must really not have occurred to him before that Chubb might have advised Lord —— on the strength of what he learnt in D.O.R.R.S.

Lord —— glanced round the table with a powerful, dominating, provocatively self-satisfied look. I was certain he knew exactly what he had done.

For a moment everyone was still. Chubb was looking down at his papers, James was holding a gold pencil against his chin, Robert was watching Sir Francis.

Suddenly Chubb began to speak. I gave him great credit for it. True, it was his only chance – and not really a serious chance – but he took it with unusual spirit. He was fighting desperately, and in the strain of great emotion his face looked quite different. He seemed to be holding his head a little further back, so that he could only just see over the top of his spectacles, and his eyes looked smaller.

'I think the time has come when I must make my position clear,' he said, 'otherwise I can see the way open to grave misconstruction being put upon my actions. As I've already said, and I can't say it more strongly, at no time did I consciously overstep the bounds of security, in connection with the survey of firms I undertook for D.O.R.R.S. I agree with Lord ——, and, I'm afraid, not with Sir Francis, that the firms knew a good deal about the A 16 before I ever got there.'

Chubb paused, and to my surprise took out his handkerchief and wiped his nose: yet he appeared not to notice what he was doing and went on speaking.

'The next thing is this – I'm afraid what Lord —— has just told you may make it look to some people as if I advised him, not as a personal friend, which is what I did advise him as, but as a member of D.O.R.R.S., so making use of my official position in an improper way. I think at a time like this, the best thing – it's the only thing I can do – is to lay my cards quite frankly on the table, so that you can judge for yourselves. I may say that in my own mind my conscience is perfectly clear. And in particular I want to say that I have never felt, in anything I did, that I was being in any way disloyal to D.O.R.R.S. I know that in the first place I was sent to you by my parent department because they believed in the A 15 and they were under the impression that D.O.R.R.S. believed in the A 16 – '

He was interrupted by exclamations of passionate dissent, from Sir Francis who was still officially impartial, and James Irskine, who still obtusely believed the case for the A 16 not yet fully established.

'I came to D.O.R.R.S. with every intention of remaining completely impartial, and with every intention of being loyal to my new department. I acquired as many facts about the situation as I could. As time went on I couldn't help coming round to the D.O.R.R.S. position myself. I decided that the A 16 was what we had got to concentrate on.' He made a gesture towards Robert. 'Even if Sir Francis hadn't made up his mind, I knew that Robert was quite certain, and I agreed with him.'

Robert showed no sign that he heard.

'I decided that the A 16 was what we had to concentrate on, and that the future of the country might well depend on our getting it in hand as rapidly as possible. It was my personal opinion – D.O.R.R.S. had no official opinion. It was my personal opinion that Lord —— asked for, and I felt bound to give it.'

I could not help glancing covertly at Robert to see how he was taking it. We had surmised rightly what Chubb was aiming at in the later stages of his tour, but we had not imputed motives as entirely high-minded as this – not that we necessarily believed them when we heard them.

Chubb was roused to strong emotion. 'I believed in my personal opinion and I think it was right. I think Lord —— was right in coming to his similar decision. But I'll only say I think I was right, because we can't say yet who'll turn out in the end to be right. But I'm willing to let history be my judge.'

He was a genuinely humble man. Yet he could not help repeating it, his newly-found phrase: 'I'm willing to let history be my judge.'

'Following upon Sir Francis,' added Lord ——. It was his first cheap remark and it sheared him of some of his authority and power. There was something empty about him after all.

'I think,' said Sir Francis, with admirable gravity, 'that is all that remains to be said.'

The meeting was over. Sir Francis caught Dr Chubb's eye. 'Are you returning to your office?' It meant that he proposed to collogue further with Chubb on his own.

As I stood up I noticed the K.Y.M.S. on my blotting-pad. I grinned at Robert and at James and they looked surprised. They did not realise that they too had said barely a word.

We went out of the room, leaving Sir Francis to exchange the last civilities with Lord ——. Robert and I put on our overcoats in silence, although there was no-one to overhear our conversation. Our thoughts were in accord. We were both convinced that the upshot of Chubb's activities was laudable and reassuring. That there might have been some conspiracy between him and Lord —— did not really worry us. But we knew that it would worry Sir Francis. It would shock him to such an extent that he would not be able to help acting upon it.

For the most sensible of his rather doubtful manoeuvres in D.O.R.R.S., Chubb was going to be sacked.

CHAPTER IX

MEDITATIONS

In our activities there was a lull that began with days and stretched out into weeks.

Outside, everything changed. The snow suddenly disappeared from the streets and squares. The sun shone constantly and people complained of the warmth. Spring had come.

In Parliament Square the old book-stall pill-box was cleared away and workmen were slowly laying out the ground afresh with grass and arc-shaped flower-beds. Walking through the square at lunch-time we saw sunlight flashing on the glossy feathers of birds perched on the head of Abraham Lincoln's statue, and gleaming on the coloured mosaic roof of the little Victorian gothic monument that reminded me of the Albert Memorial and whose name I never knew – it has gone now.

And as Robert and I strolled in St James's Park before going back to the office we had not much new to talk about. There were odd days of interest, when Sir Francis presented his report to the inter-departmental committee, and when Dr Chubb left us.

Until the time of his departure Chubb was occupied in writing something. Through a small space where the buckram lining had been stripped from the window of his office door, we could see him as we passed. He sat very still, holding his head on one side and slightly back, so as to look through his spectacles, endlessly writing.

'What can it be?' I said.

'*The New Prince*', said Robert, without hesitation.

And then, one day, his office was empty.

'He hasn't been with us long, has he, sir?' said Froggatt, as if he knew nothing about it whereas he really knew everything. He paused and then said respectfully: 'It will, of course, give us a little more accommodation. Would you object if I moved some of the staff round a bit?'

No startling decision was reached that spring about the A 16s. We knew that in due course the A 16 would be made, but such changes in affairs do not come about so much by sudden big strokes as by the accumulating pressure of a lot of little ones. Not now, was the rule: in due course.

There was no development in my relationship with Myrtle. For days and then weeks I did not hear from her. I had expected an unrestrainedly affectionate letter from her on her return home after Sir Francis's party. No letter came. I was at first surprised and then puzzled. I waited. I received a couple of notes with a week's interval between them. I did not write to her – at first I did not know why. And then, as I noticed that I was falling back into my old state of jarring anxiety, I realised the truth. Our momentary drawing-together was of no significance. The old battle of wills was on again, as fiercely and as lastingly as ever.

What was happening between Robert and Julia, I did not know. He saw her frequently, and we talked a good deal about her, but his reticence and evasiveness made me feel that he was keeping something to himself. On several points I had no doubt. Firstly, Robert had decided not to marry Julia, although I was not certain Julia did not believe that somehow or other she could still bring him to it. Secondly, Julia was sleeping with Jocelyn Plumer; and thirdly she was regularly seeing Wladislaw – for the purpose of quarrelling violently with him.

I was haunted by a phrase that had struck me in one of Robert's novels – 'the naked clash of selves.' I was tempted to see all our divided loves and hates in terms of it. What did we all want and why did we all not get it? What overthrew us when we were at last settling for a decent compromise? We were at the mercy of stirring, ravenous selves, whose power even reason and affection could barely mitigate. No wonder we suffered. With those who were dearest to us, with those to whom we most wanted to abandon ourselves – the naked clash of our demands to possess.

I observed that Robert, Julia, Myrtle and I had all fallen back into our old pattern of behaviour. The March breezes blew round St James's Park, rippling the lake and waving the bare iris leaves. The ducks with dark satiny green heads waddled, quacking, along the gravel. I was struck by a longing to escape from the pattern. I knew what I wanted to do. I wanted to start writing a novel. It was unbearable not to be able to.

One day Robert and I were standing on the suspension bridge. It was quivering as people walked across in threes and fours. We were looking towards the pale grey towers and roofs of the Horse Guards and the Home Office. Whitehall. *A propos* of nothing, Robert said:

'We've got to think about getting out of this.'

I knew exactly what he meant. If only we could! I felt a wave of excitement, and of longing to get down to it.

CHAPTER X

A TOTALLY IRRELEVANT INCIDENT

One evening I came home to find the front door of my house bolted. I rang and for a few minutes – there was no reply. My first thought was that I had been locked out for moral turpitude, though it seemed rather belated because I had not had Myrtle up in my rooms for over a month. While I stood in the porch I saw the curtains of a ground-floor window moving. A moment later I heard the bolts being drawn and Mrs Burdup opened the door.

She closed the door behind me and shot the bolts back again.

I stared at her. 'Will you come inside for a moment, Mr Lunn?' She led me through her eavesdropper's door. She said: 'I've got something to tell you.' It was quite unnecessary to say that.

She sat down on the edge of an arm-chair. Her face was normally fresh-complexioned – there was nothing unhealthy about her meanness and ladylikeness. Her complexion now looked fresher. Her eyes seemed wider open, her thin mouth was trembling. She was twisting one of her rings round and round.

'This morning I had a mysterious telephone call. It was a man's voice. He said "Is that Mrs Burdup?" and I said "Yes", and then he said "You've read about all these murders in the newspapers recently? Well, you're the next on the list." And then he rang off.'

I said promptly: 'It was somebody playing a practical joke on you.'

She said: 'I don't know anybody who would.'

I took this to be true. She seemed to have no friends or even friendly acquaintances – I had never seen anyone visiting her.

'That isn't all. This afternoon he rang again. It was the same voice. This time he said: "If you'll do what I say, I may let you off for a little while." Those were the exact words. I said "I'd like you to say that to my maid. She's standing here beside me." And he rang off again. I nearly fainted.'

I said: 'Ah, somebody's pretending they're going to blackmail you. You don't need to be afraid.'

'I rang up the police straight away. An inspector came from Scotland Yard. He asked me a lot of questions, and he said he'd come again.' She was breathless with agitation. 'He says they have ways of tracing telephone calls.' She swallowed. 'There was another call as soon as he'd gone. I thought I really would faint if I heard the voice again. . . I got the maid to answer it. When he heard it wasn't me he cut off.'

She was terrified. I had always thought she was a hateful person and I genuinely found it hard to feel sorry for her. For a murderer the telephonist seemed to have made an unusually sensible choice.

Mrs Burdup then gave a long list of precautions she was taking. One of the lodgers was going to sleep in a camp-bed outside her bedroom door. Locks and bolts were to be installed – no lodger was to come in after midnight, a rule which she had been trying to find a good reason for enforcing as long as I had known her. And so on.

At last I got away from her. As I walked along the darkened corridor into the hall, the telephone rang. It made me jump. I took off the receiver and said: 'This is Lunn speaking!' There was a click, and then silence.

Mrs Burdup made a choking noise. I had to go back again and stand by while she made herself some tea – much stronger than any she ever served me for breakfast.

Finally I went up to my room for the night. I did not believe anybody wanted to murder Mrs Burdup. I did believe somebody wanted to torment her. I did not believe the man was a complete stranger. I was sure it was somebody who knew her well.

Just as I was falling asleep an inspiration brought me wide awake. The man was her husband. It was Burdup.

I recalled that Mrs Burdup had never actually told me she was a widow. And next morning I had a long conversation with the maid, who fixed me with a shrewd cynical Cockney eye and said: 'I bet I know who it is. It stands to sense, don't it?..' She shook her head. 'It's 'er 'usband. Come back.'

The mystery was never solved as far as I knew. The calls came at irregular intervals and were never traced. I got the impression that Scotland Yard had not seen fit to concentrate their entire energies on the case. Mrs Burdup remained terrified, but her terror was dissipated gradually as she ventured further from the house and was not garrotted. If she knew who it was, then the fact that she never told anybody merely strengthened my belief.

I had reflected on how the phases of my life, of Robert's and Julia's and Myrtle's, fell into a recurrent pattern. Mrs Burdup's did not. This affair was totally irrelevant. Burdup had done something completely fresh.

I asked myself how I could ever hope to understand what people were like.

CHAPTER XI

THE LETTER

One morning a long letter came at last from Myrtle. It said:

Dear Joe,

I do not know how to begin this letter to you – I have delayed writing it for so long because I did not know how to break it to you, but I realise that it can't go on any longer. You must have realised already what I am trying to say. Please forgive me, darling.

I don't know if I'm doing the right thing or not, but I have decided that whatever happens I can't really leave Dennis. I know how much you need me, darling, but somehow the break with him is something I can't bring myself to do. You know how much I long to come to you, but there is something that holds me to him no matter how I tell myself I should be happier if he gave me my freedom. It is terribly hard to explain it to you, because I don't really know how to explain it to myself. I think it's really that Dennis and I have had seven years of married happiness, and seven years of married happiness is too much to sacrifice.

I have thought about it for so long now that I feel I could go on writing to you so long that you would be bound to understand, only I am so terribly tired and worn out by it all. I expect you will have guessed how unhappy I have been through all these months since Dennis came back. I hardly seem to have slept at all. One cannot go on being torn in two indefinitely, and it made it so much worse to see that I was making you and Dennis so unhappy too. You will never know how utterly wretched I have been.

However it's all over now, and I can start trying to live a normal life again. It is such a great consolation that Dennis has forgiven me. I feel I have got so much to make up for to him. Please darling don't think I've been persuaded to do this against my will. When I think of the seven years married happiness that I had almost forgotten I know that I cannot sacrifice it even for you, darling. I feel dreadful about it and I can only hope that perhaps in time you will be able to forgive me as Dennis has done. Will you?

I am sorry I have smudged this letter, but I am crying as I write it.

My father is still seriously ill.

      Myrtle

I took the letter with me to the office and gave it to Robert to read.

He handed it back.

'You won't reply, of course.'

I shook my head to signify No.

CHAPTER XII

ANNOUNCEMENT IN *THE TIMES*

R obert came into the office holding a copy of *The Times* – I took a different newspaper. He opened it, folded it back and laid it before me. I read the column of forthcoming marriages.

CAPTAIN J. PLUMER AND MISS J.C. DELANEY
The engagement is announced between Captain Jocelyn Plumer, Coldstream Guards, only son of Sir Francis Plumer, Bt., of 34 Chester Street, S.W.1., and Julia Christina, youngest daughter of the late Dr S. Delaney and of Mrs S. Delaney of W. Kensington.

I exclaimed. Robert made no comment.
'It'll never come off,' I said.
'No.'
I said: 'She'll go back to Wladislaw in the end.'
Robert nodded.

CHAPTER XIII

THE END

There we were, all four of us, back where we started.

Myrtle's letter caused me rage and misery, although, to be honest, my predominant feeling at first was relief. It was all over. I did not expect to see her ever again.

And then I ran into Myrtle by chance in Regent Street, about three weeks after getting her letter. She was alone and I detached myself from the friends I was with. She was dressed in black and looking woebegone.

'My father's dead,' she said.

I condoled as sincerely as I could.

She looked at me as if she were going to burst into tears: 'I keep seeing you in the street, from the tops of buses...'

I felt quite cut off from her. She might be wishing she had changed her mind, but I was determined to have no more of it. When she had gone away, phrases from her letter kept recurring to me.

'Seven years of married happiness.'

'It's such a great consolation that Dennis has forgiven me.'

Even a saint, I felt, might have been a little ruffled by such nonsense – and it really was stained with her tears, showing that people can cry as readily over the false as the true.

I thought Robert had accepted his lot rather more easily, possibly because he had never been so deeply involved and so unreservedly hopeful. He remained very fond of Julia and she of him. Wladislaw resented their friendship, while not attempting to destroy it because he thought Robert was the only man who had a good influence on Julia – which conclusion I suspected Wladislaw had reached the more easily because Robert was the only man who was not trying to get into bed with her.

The friendship of Myrtle and Julia lapsed, though Myrtle kept in touch, against Haxby's wishes, with Robert. A really extraordinary thing happened: Myrtle met The Headlamps and they struck up an intimate relationship. As far as we could gather their bond was a great romantic love they had each lost.

Jocelyn Plumer disappeared from our story as suddenly as he had entered it. His engagement to Julia was formally broken and he married the sister of one of his friends. Sir Francis, for all his courteous manners, could not disguise his relief.

The office of D.O.R.R.S. was in due course merged with another division, and Sir Francis, because he was just about to retire, they said officially, was not made its boss. It made us sad. James Irskine was promoted and so was Froggatt: to that we were neutral.

However, when the changes in the D.O.R.R.S. were made, Robert and I were elsewhere. I have observed that we were all back where we started, battered perhaps, but undaunted. Somehow Robert and I had been carried a stage nearer to our goal.

One Saturday afternoon in the middle of spring we were walking in Kew Gardens. It was impossible to believe that the winter had been so hard. On the rolling green slopes there were thousands of daffodils and narcissi in bloom. The air was still and warm. People were strolling happily beneath the trees and round the lake.

Something made me recall Myrtle, and in spite of the sunshine a heavy, sad, reflective mood fell upon me. My first feeling of relief at the break had long since disappeared, and as the weeks passed I felt a tide of loneliness and despair rising. My irritation with her had dwindled, and now I dreamed of what I had missed. Myrtle might feel she had lost the great romantic love of her life, but I knew at the bottom of my heart that I had come off worst. It was a strange reversal that time had brought about. Who would have thought, I wondered, on seeing my first affair with Myrtle, with its youthful gaiety and carelessness, its bitter-sweet ending in my coming off best, that eight years would reduce me to this wretched conclusion? It seemed to me that Myrtle would not be seriously unhappy. Really she was a rather ordinary girl: somehow she would fit into the comfortable pattern of life. While I, though I might have had my own way for a little time at the beginning, was going to have to pay for an awkward temperament before I finished. At last I glimpsed my fate. I cannot say I liked the look of it.

We paused before a magnolia tree. The flowers were perfect. It looked as if a swarm of stiff white butterflies had alighted simultaneously on the naked branches.

'The pink magnolias come out before the white,' I said.

Robert ignored the remark.

'What are you thinking about?' I asked.

He said: 'I think we ought to count on resigning from the office by the end of June at the latest.'

My elegiac mood was shattered.

'We've got enough money between us,' he said. I couldn't believe my ears.

Yet suddenly the day seemed brighter, the air warmer, the daffodils yellower; and the magnolias might have been just going to fly away to the sparkling sun – my spirits going with them, no more mornings before the office! No more depending on girls! Free men at last!

Well, Robert and I got down to Art. And there we were. The only possible thing you could ask me now is what did we write? Robert chose to write under a different name, which he has asked me not to give away. And so did I – but there is no secret about that.